THE DRAGON IN THE WHITES SERIES

Omnibus Volume II

BY TIM BAIRD

For permissions contact: tbaird@worcester.edu
www.timbaird.us

Paperback ISBN: 979-8-3303-1071-5
Ebook ISBN: 979-8-3303-1072-2

Book cover design and layout by
Ellie Bockert Augsburger of Creative Digital Studios.
www.CreativeDigitalStudios.com

Cover design features:
Close-up of a scaly dragon egg with intricate textures on a transparent background. Perfect for fantasy, mythical, and imaginative themes By Rattanathip/ Adobe Stock

Edited by Ellie Bockert Augsburger

Author photograph by Samantha Melanson.
www.samanthamelanson.com
Used with permission. All rights reserved.

Foreword from the Author

While writing the manuscripts for the three novels within the Dragon in the Whites series, 'The Dragon in the Whites', 'Washington's Dragon Hunter', and 'Dragon Liberator', I kept skipping over ideas for fun scenes or tangential sub-stories to keep the manuscript on track and prevent it from becoming a 200,000-word book. They were cast into the aether, sentenced to live out their existence as fleeting memories of tales never told in the back of my mind.

After finishing the third novel, however, I felt compelled to let those stories out and share them with you, the reader. I hope that their telling will round out the stories more smoothly, fill in some plot gaps, and help you learn more about the individual characters. Whatever role they fill for you individually as you read them, I hope that you have fun diving back into my dragon world and enjoy the following text.

As always, I appreciate your continued love and support.

Enjoy!

Tim

TABLE OF CONTENTS

THE TINKERER

Flipping the sun visor back up to the ceiling of the cab and looking to the sky, Captain Devin Gage knew that this wasn't going to be a normal call. Scanning the air above Mount Greylock, he saw quickly dashing blurs of color dart back and forth across his field of view. It was hard to see what they were, but he had a sinking feeling that the rumor mill around the station might be true this time.

Looking back to the road, he gripped the steering wheel tighter and readied himself for the intersection ahead. Honking the horn, he gave the drivers ahead a little advanced notice.

"Hey Sean!" he shouted to the new recruit on the seat next to him. "You want to give that siren a pull?"

Grinning, the volunteer firefighter reached up to the line and gave it a tug. The siren blared throughout the sleepy town of Cheshire, sending cars before them to pull over and get out of the way.

"Never gets old!" Devin shouted, trying to keep the enthusiasm up. He couldn't let the recruit see how worried he really was. The captain had spent years in and around western mass slinging hoses and putting out all manners of fires during his career. But dragons? That was something new for him.

Swinging wide to the left first, he spun the steering wheel clockwise and pulled the truck to the right, propelling the truck and men up West Mountain Road. White-knuckling his way up the old road, the captain struggled to keep the truck going straight while at top speed. While his truck may be on the lighter side, it was still an effort to launch the twenty tons of steel and water around the twisty turns of the mountain road.

"Coming up on Rockwell," Gage spoke into the radio. "Hang on!"

Working the stick through its gears, he slowed the truck down as low as he was comfortable to keep the mechanical beast from rolling sideways during the turn without wasting too much time. Seeing the road straighten out ahead of his windshield, he mashed the gas pedal and began working his way up through the gears once more. He needed to get his rig and the rest of the team up the mountain road as quickly as possible, but if he were to wreck the truck on the way, he would block the road for traffic going both up and down the mountain. It wouldn't pay to rush more than necessary, even if the risk seemed worth it.

Gritting his teeth, he settled into fourth gear and into a steady speed of forty miles per hour. Seemingly slow, but that was fast for a truck of its size on a road such as Rockwell. Watching the curve ahead, Gage relied on years of driving experience to guide his hands along the wheel. This was his region and he had driven this road more times than he could recall. They were almost there.

"Engine Five, Engine Five, come in," a voice rang from the radio. It was Jules back at the station.

Grabbing the mouthpiece, he called back, "This is Engine Five. Over."

"Engine Five, what's your location?"

"Engine Five on approach to Rounds Rock Trail," Gage responded. "ETA two minutes to the peak. Over."

"Roger, Engine Five. Stay safe out there. You have some nervous rangers and hikers up at the top in need of help."

"Roger, Jules. On our way."

Pressing the accelerator just a little bit more, Gage tried to coax more speed out of the old truck. These old roads weren't supposed to take this much weight, especially at higher speeds, so if he made it out of this, he'd probably get chewed out by some civil engineer on the town or state DPW. He could deal with that later. Looking over to his partner, he gave the younger man a crooked smile.

"Hey! You're not afraid of dragons, are you?"

"Ha! Dragons? What the heck are you talking about, Captain?"

"Didn't you hear the buzz going around town before we left the station?" Captain Gage said, putting some artificial mirth into his tone. He was dreading their arrival to the top but couldn't let it show. "Some people are claiming that there are dragons flying around up on top of the mountain. That they saw big, winged lizards swooping around over the town. Scary, toothy monsters shooting flames and stealing farm animals. Sounds rather fantastical to me."

"No way, sir," the recruit said, with a smirk. "I used to play D&D as a kid, but I haven't touched that stuff in years. I think that people have overactive imaginations sometimes and watch too many movies."

"Or they don't read enough books," Gage replied. "The world would be a little better if most people turned their screens off from time to time and stuck their nose into some more books."

"But then you'd have people reading about dragons and thinking that they're real!" Sean shouted, trying to be heard over the roar of the big diesel engine.

Gripping the wheel tightly, Gage held on with his left hand while downshifting to third. They were approaching some tighter turns and he needed to slow the red behemoth down. Taking the truck through the turns, he straightened out and set them on the final approach to the top of the mountain. Just a few more thousand feet and they'd be to the loop leading into the parking lot.

"True," he started, "but then they'd also read books teaching them that dragons weren't real and that most of these hokey monsters people claim to see are merely natural creatures and phenomenon that we simply don't fully understand yet. It's a big world out there and most people know nothing about it."

The recruit looked slyly over at his captain. "Firefighters are a lot deeper than I've been led to believe. Talking with Sergeant Luzgin back there..."

Gage cut him off. "Don't you believe anything that you hear out of those town cops. If it weren't for pulling over speeders on Route 2, they'd have nothing else better to do around here."

"Aren't you two friends?"

Gage smiled and waved him off. Looking back to the road, he was about to radio the rest of his team when the unit crackled to life on the dashboard. "Engine Five, Engine Five, this is Luzgin behind you. Be on the lookout for unidentified units on foot beyond the next turn. The chopper is reporting something big coming through the trees in front of your position. Over."

"This is Engine Five, Roger."

Thanks, Luzgin, he thought to himself.

Turning to the recruit to tell him to keep his eyes peeled, he saw the shadow leap from the underbrush on the right side of the road and leap out into the road. Pressing the clutch pedal into the floor and slamming on the brakes, Gage held on with all his might as the firetruck's momentum fought against the straining brake calipers trying to halt their rotation. The truck's back end slid out behind them to the left, sending the vehicle into an angled slide up the road. Between the rough surface of the road, the brakes, and the fact that they were going uphill, Gage was just barely able to bring the truck to a stop without rolling over.

As he felt the passenger side tires touch back down onto the asphalt, he realized just how close they really had come to biting it. With his lungs working overtime sending air back and forth through his trachea, he stared through the dust hanging in midair just outside of his windshield. There before him, just ten feet away, was the largest black bear that he'd ever seen in his life. While not an avid hunter himself, he had an uncle who actively hunted bear, so he was familiar with what constituted a normal body size.

"Look at the size of that thing!" Gage blurted out in between breaths.

The two men watched the bear slowly walk closer to the truck in the middle of the road, seemingly fearless of the giant red monstrosity. How a bear, a completely wild animal, should seem to be unafraid of such a sight, was unknown to the two men. Either that, or the bear was confident that it could win a fight between the two if presented with an opportunity.

Loosening his grip on the steering wheel, the captain moved his hand toward the center and gave the horn a long honk. Finding the truck's brand's logo, he gave the piece a quick push to blare the horn. If his intention was to scare the animal away, he was dead wrong. The bear growled towards the truck and continued to step closer. Opening its massive jaws, the creature let loose a blood-curling roar, looking straight into Gage's eyes.

"Sean," he whispered. "Lock your door, will ya?" Hearing the recruit depress the button on the side of the panel, he added, "And grab your axe."

"Engine Five, this is Engine One in the rear of the procession," a new voice blurted through the radio speaker. "What seems to be the holdup?"

"Ah, we encountered a little bit of wildlife up here. Nothing to be worried about." Releasing his finger from the 'Talk' button on the radio, he turned to Sean. "Hit that siren a few times. Let's see what that does."

The recruit flicked the switch for the automatic siren to run and leaned back in his seat. Watching the bear's reaction, it was clear that they were only making the situation worse.

"What do you want to do, Captain?"

"We'll just drive forward and make it get out of the way," Gage replied. "I have no desire to run a wild bear over with my truck, but we need to get to the top of this road and fast."

Putting the truck back into first gear, he was about to hit the gas when he saw a rustling in the bushes to the right. While focusing on the cluster of branches shaking violently several feet from the bear, a blur of motion rocketed from the greenery and descended upon the mass of black fur and muscle. Unable to believe his eyes, Gage realized that he was watching a dragon devour the bruin while it was still alive.

The dragon (at least he believed it was a dragon as he'd never seen a real one before and was merely working with what he knew from the rumors and radio calls) had pounced upon the back of the bear and was actively gorging itself upon the guts of the creature. Pinning its limbs to the ground, the dragon dove his tooth-lined maw into the steaming flesh of the carcass over and over again.

"Sir?"

"I know."

"What the he..."

"Screw it," Gage said, dropping the clutch and mashing the gas pedal with his heavily-booted right foot. The fire truck groaned back to action and the back wheels chirped on the sun-warmed asphalt. Accelerating up the hill toward their target, the dragon was now in charge of its own destiny and could choose to flee... or meet its doom.

They closed the gap in a matter of seconds, watching intently as the dragon glared the driver down in the process. Unleashing a furious salvo of fire towards the grille of the vehicle, the dragon wasted its chance to move out of the way. The hulking mass of the truck drove the polished steel bumper into its draconian skull. Dragon and bear alike were slammed forward a dozen feet and into the blacktop. Gage never relented and kept accelerating the engine towards his target. Approaching the dazed creature, he veered to the left and aimed to hit the creature again with the right corner of the truck's bumper.

As the roar of the diesel engine approached the prone figure on the road, Gage shifted the transmission down a gear to get additional torque out of the Cummins inline-six. Gripping the steering wheel tightly, he braced himself physically and emotionally. He had never killed a creature such as this before, and almost regretted it. Almost. He needed to protect the men and women under his command, and there were innocent civilians up the road who needed his help. Watching the last few feet of asphalt disappear below his bumper, he slammed into the dragon one last time, sending its pummeled body up and over the guard rail on the right.

Feeling the drag of the bear's body underneath, Gage smashed the gas pedal again and managed to get the truck to bounce up and over the mangled carcass. He felt terrible, especially for the disgrace to the bear's remains, but he'd worry about that later.

"Sir, did you see the… the… the creature back there?"

"Roger. Creature sighted and neutralized," Gage replied flatly to the driver of one of the trucks in the middle of the procession. "Ignore and proceed to the target. Arrival in one minute."

Shifting gears again, Gage coaxed a little more speed out of the aging engine and rocketed it up the hill. Lowering his chin to the steering wheel, he looked below the edge of the windshield trying to see more of the sky above. He saw shadows continue to dart back and forth above the canopies of the trees, causing the knot in his stomach to twist furiously. Reaching down, he grabbed the microphone again and pressed the 'Talk' button.

"Hey Luzgin, switch to two-player mode."

Pausing a moment, he waited a few moments for her to switch channels. Changing over to their usual private channel, he ignored the confused look that he could see coming from the recruit in the corner of his eye.

"Hey Luzgin, you there?"

"Roger," her voice returned, thankfully.

"You seeing all of this?"

"You mean the ginormous black bear that just ran in front of you? Or the fire-breathing flying lizards orbiting our airspace? Or the dragon that you hit with your truck?"

He grinned at her blatant sarcasm. He could always count on her to give him crap back, especially when off the record.

"Yes."

"Then yes, I saw all of that," she responded, the concern evident in her tone. "What do you want to do?"

"We drive," he returned, confidently. "There's not much else that we can do. There are people up there counting on us. Regardless of these mythological monstrosities, there are blazing fires, an exploded lodge, and probably injured people to rescue. We owe them our best efforts."

"Roger, sir."

Listening to her acknowledgement through the radio, he could tell that she probably didn't fully agree with them blindly rushing into the scene unprepared. She was no coward and would die trying to protect the people of her town but wouldn't want to make the sacrifice foolishly nor in vain.

"But don't be stupid about it," he added. "Keep your head on a swivel and stay low."

Giving the truck a little more gas, he urged the thing up the hill towards their destiny. He wasn't sure what they were about to encounter, but he could confidently say that none of them were ready for it. Finally reaching their destination, Gage brought the roaring vehicle around the final curve in the road and slammed on the brake pedal as hard as he could. Tossing the stick into neutral, he twisted the wheel to the left and brought the engine to a nail-biting, tire-thrashing sideways screeching halt before a roadblock of grey stone and broken glass. Holding himself to his left, Gage felt the truck's weight fall back to the left side wheels as the mass of the truck finally came to rest. Looking out the window, he couldn't tell what he was looking at.

"What is all this mess?"

"That's, uh, the tower, I think," the recruit replied, "Sir."

Glancing around, Gage realized for the first time since their approach to the peak that the Veteran's Tower, was, in fact, completely absent from the top of the mountain. Looking around at the rubble surrounding them, he mentally added the volume of debris and concluded that this must be the tower's remains. Grabbing the radio's microphone, he quickly called out orders for his team.

"Luzgin! Send a car back down to the bottom and secure the entrance. Don't let anyone up or down the road without clearance or a damn good reason."

"Yes, sir!"

"Lutes! Plow through the debris and bodies to get as close to the buildings as possible. Put out the fires and save what we can."

"Bodies, sir?"

"You'll see when you get up here," he started, personally

disgusted at his command's implication but doing what needs to be done. "They're not human. Just do it."

"Yes, sir."

"Lenny! Call the DPW and tell them that we need to clear the rubble from the memorial. Get a bulldozer, loader, and a dump truck up here. Have them queue up at the bottom and wait for the all-clear signal before driving up the road."

Looking around at the destruction before him, he reconsidered his request.

"Actually, Lenny," he said, scanning the rubble in front of the trucks. "Send the bulldozer up now. Let's get this crap out of the way for our trucks."

"Yes, sir!"

Hanging the radio back on its hook, he threw open the door to the truck and hopped down to the pavement below. Feeling the crunch of the stone rubble beneath his boots, he picked his way through the larger chunks as he advanced towards the center of the peak. Seeing the chaos in front of him, he turned back and walked along the length of the truck until he got to the tool racks. Reaching up, he grabbed the two axes hanging there and hefted one in each hand.

Looking over his shoulder to Sean and the rest of the team behind him, he motioned for them to hug the left side of the road to make room for the trucks coming up the road. Walking over to meet up with the recruit, he handed the young man his spare axe.

"What's this for, sir?" The young man inquired, looking confused. "I don't see any buildings barred or trees needing to be felled to minimize fire spread."

Shuddering at the grim thought, he didn't want to share his rationale with the man just yet.

"Let's hope that you won't need it," he said, looking over at the man with a stark expression on his normally cheerful face. "Keep your eyes open and be ready for anything."

Rounding the truck, he scanned the battlefield for any dangers. Far off in the distance, he could see some commotion brewing by two huge dragon bodies. A black dragon and a green dragon, laying adjacent to each other, appeared to be dead or in the process of expiring. Several people huddled nearby. Off to his right, the trucks were trying to drive through the confusion, pushing dragon and bear bodies out of the way and driving over what they could. Blocks of gray stone littered their paths and posed a possible tire-popping risk.

"Hopefully the damn bulldozer gets here soon", he muttered under his breath.

Hearing some voices off to his right, he gripped the handle of his axe tightly as he tried to catch sight of the newcomers. Coming through a copse of trees, he was thankful to see a group of people heading their way. They looked to be scared stiff, but visibly uninjured from this distance. Turning to several of his men in the rear of the column, he motioned for them to go join the cluster of people being led by a man and a woman.

"Aargh!"

Whipping around, he found Sean pinned to the ground by a small red dragon. The creature was no bigger than a common dog and had the young man pinned to the ground. Its head reared back and forth, trying to find access to its prey's fleshy bits. Sean, to his credit, was doing an admirable job holding the creature's head at bay, having shoved the axe handle below its chin and wrestling a leg free in a vain attempt to kick the body away from him. Almost getting his arms to straighten out, he was actively trying to bench-press the tooth-filled mouth up and away from his face before the hungry creature could have a chance to finish its attack.

Without stopping to think any further, Gage took two power strides and leapt through the air, swinging his axe up and over his head in midflight. Coming down just to the side of his partner, he brought the axe head down upon the neck of the dragon whelp. The sharpened blade (normally kept on hand to break down locked doors, fell trees, or rip holes in the roofs of burning buildings) was called upon to handle a dire task. His partner's life, or death, now hung in the balance and was directly tied to the performance of the axe and its wielder.

Lodging deep into the scale-covered flesh of the winged horror, the creature spasmed uncontrollably, but still had the fortitude to continue its attack. It's clawed hands and feet persisted in their attempts to grab and slash the pinned man while its head sought the path of least resistance to its food. Reaching forward, Gage planted a rubberized boot against the creature's side and wrenched the axe free from the bulging muscles of the dragon. Taking a deep breath and strengthening his grip on the wooden handle, he brought the sharpened steel up and around once more, aiming straight for the previous wound. Striking true, the firefighter crunched into the spinal column of the dragon's neck and cleaved the appendage from the rest of its body.

Jumping back in disgust, he kicked out his foot and launched the headless body from the still pinned recruit. The severed head landed in a wet thump upon the young man's chest. Scrambling backwards, the young man scrambled back on his hands and feet to escape the drooling, bloody head of the beast. The disembodied head rolled to the grass below. Despite the chaotic noises resounding from the air above as the dragons continued to fly back and forth, the sloppy squish of flesh could be heard by everyone nearby. As the head finally lost the remainder of its kinetic energy and succumbed to gravity's will, the face pointed towards Gage. The dragon's dead eyes and still deadly teeth glared up at him from the ground, compelling him to kick the bloody mess out of the way and into the nearby bushes.

Extending a hand to Sean, he helped the lad to his feet and away from the mess below. The man was covered in blood and drool from the maw of the snarling beast and was quite a sight for the experienced firefighter. He had spent years battling fires and rescuing people from some of the dirtiest environments around, but he had never seen a person as badly in need of a shower as the recruit did just then. Contrary to the general mood and ever-present dangers that surrounded them, Gage couldn't help but laugh.

"Sean, you alright?" he managed after the errant chuckles subsided.

Still in shock from the incident, Sean looked down at himself and nodded. "I think so, sir," he said. "I think that I just need a new jacket."

"Hah!" Gage bellowed. "And probably a clean pair of pants. Hustle back to the truck and grab a spare suit from the backseat of the cab. Come back out and join us when you're ready and have caught your breath. Sit down for a minute and drink some water, while you're over there."

Thanking him, the recruit ran back to the truck and away from the dead dragon. Happy with how the skirmish ended, Gage had to remind himself that the kid came very close to being killed back there. They weren't out of this just yet. Surveying the scene, he noticed a person walking towards the young people huddled around the large green dragon corpse up ahead. Turning to the officers walking behind him, he motioned over to them, clearly conveying the need for possible intervention. As they ran past, the man and woman who had escorted the hostages before followed in their wake.

Walking along, Gage found several mangled corpses of gigantic black bears littered about with an equal number of dragons. Glancing up to the sky, he noticed that the orbiting dragons from before had all but departed. Only an occasional creature darted back and forth amongst the clouds now, leaving the mountain top in relative silence. Hearing a woman shouting of to the right, he looked over to see the woman from before punching the newcomer in the face, sending her backwards to the ground. He wasn't sure, but it seemed like she had a rocket launcher thrown from her hands. About to run over, he could see that the cops had the situation under control, so he resumed his patrol of the carnage.

Finding a few dragons still clinging to life, he felt obligated to help them. While they were blood-thirsty killing machines which had tried to eat his partner just a few minutes ago, they were still living creatures at the end of the day. Unfortunately, as he tried to tend to their wounds, they all wound up trying to attack him. He wanted to save them, but it wasn't worth his own life if they were going to be ungrateful about it.

"No good deed goes unpunished," he muttered as he drove the

axe head into the skull of a brown winged nightmare at his feet.

Systematically, he went from dragon to dragon, swiftly ending their suffering as humanely as possible. It took a few minutes, but he must have killed about eight of them in total. He had to put down a few bears while he was at it, feeling very sorry for their loss. While they sometimes became nuisances in the community, it was the humans who had encroached upon their home in the woods in the first place, so people couldn't complain about them trying to steal their food and upend their trash barrels in the process.

The last thought bothered him. As he killed the final dragon, bringing the mountain back to its normally calm and peaceful state, he thought about the dragons and their presence. While he had never seen a dragon before today, he had grown up assuming that they were merely myths from yesteryear. Science hadn't always been able to fully explain all of the creatures in the world and had to fill in the gaps somehow... but just how long they had really been around? Where did they come from? And why had he never heard of them before now? Clearly the government or some organization must have known about their existence, and if so, were they actively hiding them from the general public?

Shaking his head to break himself from going too far down this thought spiral and going into a full-blown conspiracy theory rant, he took stock of the area around him. The dragons were all dead or gone, the bears likewise. The cops had secured that crazy woman with the rocket launcher, and the hostages had been cleared from the buildings. Looking around, he couldn't see the four newcomers who had been attacked by the woman near the green and black dragons.

"Whatever," he mumbled. Luzgin and her team would take care of them.

Looking around, he directed a few of the firefighters to small burn spots eating away at the remaining buildings. Seeing the bulldozer finally arrive and begin to clear the road for the trucks, he waved the awaiting trucks onward and directed them one-by-one to key areas. He watched with satisfaction as the crews scrambled out and began dousing fires within the forested area, denying the dragons their continued destruction upon the land. Nodding with as much happiness as one could have in this situation, Gage made his way back to the cab of his truck to use the radio. Smirking to Sean as the recruit hustled past him in his new suit, he jumped up into the driver's seat and grabbed the microphone.

Calling back to the station, he relayed the status and their progress so far to the dispatcher. Requesting a call to the local Air Force base, he politely reminded the dispatch team to pull out all the stops with their pleasantries to try to get at least a single fighter out here ASAP to patrol the skies and track down any airborne stragglers. He wasn't sure how many dragons were still flying around up there, but even one was dangerous. Hanging the microphone back on its base, he swung his legs out of the seat and dropped to the ground below.

Walking along the rubble-littered ground, he observed his teams working together in a smooth concert to bring order and safety back to the mountaintop. Nodding in satisfaction, he proceeded towards the site of the former memorial tower. Once a beauty to behold, he had grown up loving the sight of the glass orb and stone tower shining its light down upon the surrounding areas. But alas, it was no more. Whoever, or whatever, had taken this thing down had done a more than thorough job and left little to no evidence resembling the former structure.

"What a shame," he said to himself, walking through the rubble and kicking a few pieces aside with his steel toe boots. "This was one of my favorite places to come over the years to just sit and relax."

Shaking his head in dismay, he sat down on one of the larger flat stone blocks and rested his feet for a moment. Looking around, his team seemed to have the situation under control, and he could afford a moment of respite. Glancing down to the grass at his boots, he found himself zoning out momentarily and losing visual focus on the ground below. Staring at a shiny object off to the side as it reflected sunlight onto his face, he could feel his eyes adjust and focus on the object.

A dozen feet away, hidden amongst a pile of twisted steel,

shattered ornate glass, and broken rocks, lay some sort of mechanical device. A tinkerer by hobby, Gage had grown up loving all things mechanical and had been a pretty good machinist before falling into the firefighting career. Urging his tired knees to function, he stood up straight and walked over to the mystery object. Quickly pulling debris off from the item, he easily uncovered it within a matter of minutes. When complete, he stared down at the object before him.

There, in the grass, was a dented electrical housing about the size of an old desktop computer; a smashed transmitter of some kind; and an external power supply module. It looked to have multiple leads feeding into it. Tracing them along the ground through the rubble, he found that one had been connected to a now-destroyed gasoline-powered generator and another to the main grid. Both power cables had been severed, but from what he could tell, the wiring was salvageable.

Bending down to investigate the readout screen on the housing, he poked and prodded at a few buttons. Nothing responded, and the system appeared to be dead. There didn't seem to be an internal battery to maintain autonomous use, so he'd need to reconnect it to a power source if he were to test it out. Grabbing the components, he hefted them from the ground, grunting as he took the full weight of the device, and trudged back to the truck. Tossing everything into the back, he closed the gate with a loud clang. He could worry about that later, but for now, he needed to rejoin his team and finish cleaning up this mess.

Flicking on the lights to the basement stairs, Devin made his way down to his work bench. It had been almost a week now since the incident on top of the mountain, and he and his team had spent the past few days helping the DPW clean up the mess. The tower had been completely destroyed and was currently being reviewed by the town building inspector to determine what could be saved for possible reuse. A fundraiser had already been started online by town activists to raise money to rebuild the memorial tower as soon as possible. A team of grad students and professors from UMass Amherst had come out to begin analyzing the bodies of the dragons to determine their taxonomy.

Rumors flew around town almost faster than the dragons themselves, and he had heard stories ranging from dinosaurs returning to roam the Earth, aliens, and even government conspiracy theories about the dragons being a pet project of the Air Force. It was getting pretty ridiculous, so he hoped that whatever their true nature may be, it would come to light soon to end all of this make believe and tomfoolery.

Finally enjoying some well-deserved downtime, he had blocked off his afternoon to begin investigating the mystery device found in the rubble of the tower. It had sat on his bench for a few days as he considered just what to do with it. After tossing the parts into the back of his truck, he had initially planned on turning it over to Luzgin's team with Adams PD... but something told him to do otherwise. They had enough work on their hands, as well as a warehouse full of damning evidence for that woman whom they had captured on top of the mountain. Whoever she was, it was rumored that she was a well-connected, high-ranking official within some shadowy organization. They weren't going to miss this one little piece.

Settling in at his bench, he put on a pair of nitrile gloves and spread the individual components out. While he didn't think that there was anything toxic to the equipment, he wasn't naïve to the fact that somebody may come looking for the device at some point. If he could keep his grimy little fingerprints off the mysterious surfaces of the device, it would pay dividends later for his career and life in general. Opening a set of basic tools on his left, he got to work.

Over the next several hours, he carefully removed each panel, cover, and locking mechanism holding the thing together. He took photographs as he went, measured key dimensions, and took copious notes. He didn't know what the thing did, but if he had learned one thing over the years of tinkering and fixing old cars, it was that a good set of notes could help steer you back on course during any unforeseen *oops* moments.

When he finally had the thing taken apart, he cleared some space and set up his electrical tools. Using a power supply with multiple volt and amperage options, as well as a calibrated multimeter, he carefully went through each circuit and tested them for connectivity and assumed functionality. Thankfully, he found many of the components to be older models from mainstream sources, so a quick online search of serial numbers and labeled specs was often good enough to point him in the right direction.

It wasn't until many hours later that Devin looked up from his work and noticed the time. Already an hour past his normal bedtime, he conceded that he would need to get to sleep immediately if he were to be semi-functional at work the following day. Taking some final notes and detailed photographs of his progress, he turned off his diagnostic equipment, killed the lights on the workbench, and headed upstairs to bed.

During the following week, Devin spent several hours each night working through his electromechanical puzzle. While he still didn't know its intended purpose, he felt like he was making a lot of progress and getting closer to completion. He could just feel the finish line teasing him from around another corner or two. With each resoldered connection, replaced fuse, and upgraded wire gauge, he brought the device back up to spec and improved upon the original design in many ways.

But still... he had no clue what its ultimate function was. He didn't know what would happen when he finally powered it up for the first time. He didn't know what problem it was designed to solve; what goal its builder had in mind. All that he knew was that a broken piece of equipment had been found on his watch; it looked expensive; and had come from the heart of an epic battle. It had a great purpose in life, and he would be damned if he let whatever opportunity lay before him pass him by.

It wasn't until two weeks later that he made the final repair. He didn't know it at the time, but when the last connection was repaired and power flowed through the circuitry once more as he tested the power supply, the device came to life and resumed its diabolical operation. Feeling the cold metal thrum to life, the man sat back into his chair and watched in awe. After nearly two weeks of countless hours of work, he had finally gotten the thing to turn on.

It did nothing.

Shrugging, he moved everything away from the device, measured the temperature of a few critical components to ensure that they weren't overheating and posing a fire hazard within his home, and proceeded to walk back upstairs to his living space. Leaving the device to continue running into the long, dark night, he went to bed and tried to push the pointless hunk of metal to the back of his mind. He had a long day tomorrow and couldn't waste more time on that blasted thing when he should be sleeping like a responsible adult.

As the warm light from the LED bulbs in the basement dimmed and winked out of existence, the device sat on the bench. All alone, but finally fixed and powered up, the equipment ran through its preprogrammed subroutines and carried out the job for which it was created. Running through the motions, the power supply charged the massive bank of capacitors until they reached their limits, then shunted the power to the transmitter in a massive flow of electrical current. The transmitter, in turn, released a signal pulse along the wide band radio waves. The signal passed harmlessly through the walls and ceiling of the home, racing outward in all directions to the awaiting atmosphere beyond.

Throughout the night, the waves continued to propagate outward from the workbench, seeking any and all listeners who may heed its call. Working diligently and without pause, the equipment called out to any and all draconian minds within its operational radius.

Alone within its lair, the majestic creature stirred from its slumber. Rousing from its curled position within the protective bedding, the being's eyes met with the pitch-black atmosphere of the cave. Allowing itself a moment to adjust, the creature was able to see almost as well as during the day thanks to her dragonsight.

Stepping out of the raised edge encircling her usual sleeping spot within the rear of the lair, she stomped her clawed feet forward until she reached the mouth of the cave. Shaking the dust free from her folded wings, she stretched out her limbs as she climbed up and out of the hole in the Earth and looked out upon the dimly lit hillside. Gazing upon her domain, she was about to step out and into the cool early morning air when she heard a tremendous roar of an approaching animal. Drooping her head low, she slithered behind a rock and awaited the oncoming prey.

THUD

THUD

THUD

THUD

The vibrations through the ground drove the dragon further behind the rock, hiding her position until she was ready to strike. Rearing back, she prepared herself to lunge as a gray blur of motion passed over her head. Reeling in fright, she dropped to the sandy floor of the tunnel and waited for the beast to disappear into the distance.

Watching the poufy gray and white tail bounce down the hill and follow its owner up a tree, the dragon whelp snarled.

Another squirrel! she thought, watching the larger creature shimmy up the trunk of the far-off tree, jumping out of sight into the canopy above. *Someday I'll be bigger...*

As the commotion subsided and she found herself alone with her thoughts once more, the mysterious sense of attraction returned. Sniffing the air, she tried to locate its source but couldn't detect a tangible location. The strong pull felt like a mental urging, drawing her to a spot unknown, convincing her to drop whatever she was doing and fly away in due haste.

Emerging from the shelter of the former rabbit warren, the small dragon flexed her wings, gave them a few practice pumps, and took to the sky. Rising through the branches and leaves as she flew upwards towards the brightly illuminated Moon, she broke through the upper reaches of the canopy and found her bearings. Twisting her body to the side, she spun herself in place and pointed her eyes towards the unseen source. Not sure of what she was looking for but feeling the distant sensation that grabbed at her psyche over a week ago, she flew off into the twilight, eager to discover what lay before her.

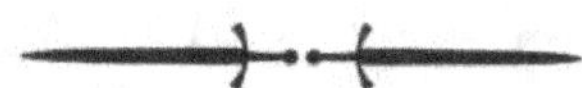

The following morning, Devin was in the kitchen preparing breakfast before heading out to work. The sounds and smells of the spattering hot bacon grease filled his soul with warmth. Even on the toughest of days, if he had a good, hearty breakfast sitting in his stomach, he could take on the world. Grabbing the toasted bread while still on the upward trajectory out of the stainless-steel toaster on the counter, he dropped the hot slices to a plate and set to buttering them.

Turning to lean against the island, he grabbed his mug of coffee and took a long sip, relishing the feeling of it coursing down his throat. Swallowing, he was in the process of bringing the ceramic vessel back to his lips when he heard a tapping sound. Looking around, he perked up his ears and tried to focus on the source. It didn't sound like any of the appliances in the kitchen, and he was most assuredly alone in his bachelor-pad apartment. Hearing the sound again, he looked to each of his windows as he was certain that the sound was coming from something tapping on glass.

Swishing the curtains out of the way with his free hand, he checked each window carefully, unsure of what would be waiting for him on the other side. He figured that it was a bird trying to get in and didn't want to scare it away, so he continued onward with caution. Making his way to the living room, he continued through his routine. He was about to go to the third window when he froze.

Raising his hand further out, he pushed the curtain all the way to the side and saw the little face looking up at him. Reaching out to place the coffee mug on the table next to him before dropping it in shock, he leaned forward until his nose was almost touching the inside surface of the windowpane. There, several inches in front of his face, was a tiny dragon. It was just like the others that he saw on top of the mountain, just proportionally smaller.

And admittedly, freakin' cute.

Staring at the little guy, he cocked his head to get a better view through the glare of the glass. As he did so, he noticed that the dragon mirrored his motion. Smirking, he tilted his head in the other direction and was amused to see the dragon follow suit. Looking past the dragon to the street beyond, he checked to see if anyone else was around. Not seeing any of his neighbors in the near vicinity, he made his decision.

Slowly reaching up to the window's lock, he carefully unlocked the latch and raised the lower sash. Watching the dragon intently as he went through the motions, he could sense a little apprehension in the young creature, but not total fear. The little one didn't fly away, if he could fly, but merely hopped back a few steps and observed him from a further distance. Waiting another moment for the dragon to settle into the new change in its environment, he proceeded to unlatch the screen and raised it upward, as well. Kneeling on the floor in front of the window, he waited.

The creature watched him intently but did not move. He could tell by the subtle motion of its nose that it was smelling the air, garnering information about him and the inside of his home. After a thorough sniffing, the dragon stepped back again and seemed content with sitting still. Admittedly disappointed, Devin tried another tack. Slowing raising his hand, he flattened his palm and held it out to the creature. Moving it slowly forward, he pass over the sill, through the window opening, and extended beyond to the outside air.

The dragon watched and waited but didn't budge. Brainstorming his options, Devin realized that he needed an edge to win the thing over. He needed bait. Slowly backing away, he held up one finger to the dragon implying that it should wait for one minute. Embarrassed by his assumption that the dragon would even remotely understand his meaning, he quickly scurried off to the kitchen in hopes of returning before the dragon ran away. Coming back around the corner, he got back to his knees and inched his way closer to the windowsill.

Ever so slowly, Devin raised his hand above the top of the painted wood sill and presented the dragon with the most tantalizing treat imaginable. As the crisp strip of hot bacon crested the sill and came into view of the tiny creature, he could see the immediate reaction dawn across its face. The little one's nose instantly perked up as the delicious aroma wafting off the meat made its way to the dragon's nostrils. The creature stood just a little taller, its neck straightened out, and it gently fluttered its small pair of wings. Leaning forward, the dragon got as close as it could without actually leaving its perch.

Sensing that he'd need to meet the dragon halfway, he slowly reached out and slide the strip of bacon from his hand and onto the wooden surface. Moving back gently, the dragon leapt from the branch of the bush that it had previously sat upon and landed on the sill ready to strike. Watching the predator hunt its prey, Devin laughed in delight as the dragon sprang upon the piece of bacon.

With four claws outstretched, the baby dragon grabbed the strip of bacon as it landed and rolled onto its back. Wrapping its tail around the end of the strip, which was almost as long as the dragon itself, the creature happily munched away at the bacon in pure delight. He had never seen a person or creature so happy to eat something in all his life. He wanted to try to reach out and try to pet the small creature, but he knew that it wasn't ready. Reaching down to his other hand, he took the second strip and broke off a tiny piece. Extending his hand slowly near the still merrily chomping dragon, he left the morsel near its head, but several inches closer to Devin himself.

Upon completing its first meal, the dragon grabbed the second piece and repeated the process. Sensing that it was growing more comfortable with Devin's presence, he reached up and repeated the process again with a third piece. As it ultimately dove into that morsel, he reached around the body of the miniature beast and closed the screen window. Looking down to its face, he noticed that the little dragon arched a brow at the action, but made no further reaction. After several more rounds of this process, Devin slowly drew the creature closer to his body until he finally got the dragon to land upon his chest for the final piece. As the dragon engaged the last bit of bacon, Devin reached out slowly, brought his hand closer to the dragon's face while with view of one of its eyes... and booped it on the nose.

The dragon let out a tiny growl, but quickly went back to eating its breakfast. Devin leaned back and laughed heartily to the point where he bounced the dragon from his chest. The creature leapt back and hovered in midair, but gently alighted onto the man's shirt after he got control of himself and stopped moving. Giving the creature a moment to resume its perch and meal, he raised his hand once more and moved it towards the creature's head. Observing its demeanor, he could tell that it was hesitant and sensed that the man was going in for another tap of its nose. Devin, not looking to scare the thing away and instead make it feel comfortable, reached up and gently pet its head.

The dragon, initially recoiling and moving low to avoid the contact, quickly leaned back into the man's hand and relished the touch. Devin continued to pet the creature, stroking its smooth scales from head to tail. Both man and dragon settled into a comfortable position and enjoyed each other's company. Not usually a pet person, Devin was pleased at how easily the dragon relaxed in his presence and accepted his friendship.

Looking down, he watched the dragon gobble up the remainder of the last piece of bacon. Looking up into his face, The creature, turning its head up to look back into his eyes, gave an imploring glance, clearly wanting more food. Devin shook his head and shrugged. While a very human expression, the dragon clearly understood and let out a tiny, almost comical sigh. Smiling, Devin almost felt bad that he didn't have more to provide for his tiny friend. He could make up some more bacon, but for now, he was happy just to sit and see what the dragon would do.

Content with its full belly, the dragon curled its tail and neck around into a circle, laid its head down upon itself, and drifted off to sleep. Staring at the small sleeping lizard, Devin breathed deeply and pondered the rest of his day. He couldn't just take the day off from work on such short notice, but he kind of wanted to stay and just hang out with the little whelp. As the moments ticked by, another thought slowly crept into his head. He initially brushed it off, but as his brain tried to think it through and rationalize the implications of his questioning thoughts, he couldn't put it off any longer. Where did this little dragon come from and were there more? And more importantly... how did it find his house?

A HAIKU

The brown moose grazes,
Delicious greens in the bog.
The dragon swoops in.

SPELUNKING

Bringing the passenger-side tires of his pickup truck onto the weed and rock slurry that was the edge of the road, Liam nosed the front of the vehicle into the low growth surrounding the thoroughfare and brought himself parallel to the edge. He hardly suspected that anyone else would dare to venture this far off the beaten path to look at the same cave in the side of the same mountain as he had just done, but if they did, he wasn't in the mood to lose a side-view mirror over it. Looking over his shoulder, he opened the door of the truck and slid his butt off the bench, dropping to the gravel below.

Leaning against the side of the truck, he stretched his aching muscles and gazed up to the rising sun. He had left his home in Manchester as early as possible to get up here before it got too hot for the day, but the long drive and his admittedly stubborn resistance to leaving his warm sheets this morning caused him to arrive just as the summer sun approached the apex of its climb across the sky. Reaching in, he grabbed his ice coffee and backpack, sliding the latter across the bench and into the impression of his tired buttocks in the cracking foam below. Opening the small pouch on the front of the pack, he extracted his well-worn copy of *Trails and Waterfalls*, quickly thumbing his way through until he found a dog-eared page.

It had been two long years since he had first read the page before him. Two long years since his entire life had been turned upside down by the events which transpired after his visit to the trail's destination.

Scanning the rumpled surface of the page, he refreshed himself on the twists and turns of the path, important landmarks to observe, and committed the key data to memory. Tossing the guide back into the zippered pouch and closing it up, he hefted the pack onto his shoulders and adjusted the straps.

His plan was to lazily walk the trail until he reached his destination and try his darned best to enjoy the trip. Actually, that's a lie. His original plan was to never come here at all and to simply live the rest of his life in seclusion where the dragon, nor the countless people online and back in his hometown, could ever find him again to torment him. And in the case of the dragon, you know, kill him. Confidence in his abilities and desire to bring this mystery to a conclusion had won out in the end. Succumbing to his goal to move forward and put this to rest, Liam decided to come and fully intended to make the best of this journey. But, like anything associated with what had transpired on that fateful day two years ago, the mere thought of going back had filled his stomach with butterflies and his veins with high pressure fluids. His head throbbed as the blood pounded the inside of his skull, threatening to tear apart his confidence should he push this too far.

Raising the stainless steel tumbler to his lips, he drained the last of the coffee, relishing the feeling of the cool liquid flowing down his throat. He felt flushed and anxious, unsure of what this day would bring and grateful to at least have a little left of his favorite drink available to him. He'd needed to remind himself to grab some Dew on the way home. You know, assuming that he wasn't attacked by a dragon again and lived to get back to his truck in one piece. There was no way that could happen twice... right?

Dropping the tumbler into the cup holder in the center console, he locked the door, fidgeted the keys into a side pouch, and hip-checked the door closed. "Might as well get this over with," he grumbled.

Twenty-odd minutes later, he found himself passing by the small pool of water where he had joyfully played with some fish and turtles two years ago. He smiled, seeing the vibrant colors of the different creatures dart back and forth through the cool, clear water. It always amazed him just how clean things were in the deep woods of Maine. Granted, Manchester could be better than some of the bigger cities down south like Boston or New York, but they couldn't shake a stick at the natural wonders of the far North. Turning back to the trail, he was happy to feel the slight presence of a bounce creep into his step. Try as hard as he might, even in this wretched place which lived rent-free in his brain for all of eternity, Liam couldn't help but have fun out here.

Rounding a bend in the trail, he emerged through a small grove of low trees and tall grasses gently swaying in the late morning breeze. Liam breathed deeply, filling his lungs with the delicious air of the woods. The untouched natural beauty of the land with its clean, cool air and water made this part of New England one of his favorite places to visit. Except for this place. Try as hard as he might, he still hated this place and could hardly believe that he had convinced himself to return.

Pulling tightly on the lower straps, he adjusted his pack and brought the weight higher on his shoulders. There wasn't much further to go from here, and he needed to be ready.

A few minutes later, he found the source of his growing anxiety. Looming before him sat the hulking hilltop housing the ill-intended cavern from. Rounding a corner in the trail, he came across a group of rocks and face to face with the gaping hole screaming at him from the mountainside. There was no sound, other than the normal chirping of birds and the gentle drone of an airplane passing by overhead in the far-off distance, but still it blasted his senses with what had transpired and what may be waiting for him just yet.

Walking closer, he meandered over to a flat boulder off the side of the trail and sat down. Taking his pack from his shoulders, he continued to stare at the opening as he fished around inside the zippered pockets. He retrieved some beef jerky and his water bottle, consciously aiming to refuel his body with energy and vital hydration before heading back into the awaiting abyss. Would he need it to get through whatever sort of shenanigans were about to befall him? If the history regarding this location was correct... he probably would.

Feeling his pulse quicken, he forced himself to slowly breathe in and out, trying to calm his body. This sucked. Well, it was going to suck. It might suck? He didn't know anymore. It was bad enough having normal teenager-type anxieties about things: girls, money, keeping his truck running, what to do after college... hell, how to get through college even remotely if that was to be his thing. Why did he need to throw *almost being killed by a dragon* into the mix? Couldn't he just live a normal life for a change?

Gulping down the barely moist hunk of overly chewed beef down his throat, he felt the dread of his past choke himself from within. Or maybe it was just the crappy, low-quality jerky. Looking back, he probably should have bought something better to snack on than the first thing he saw at the gas station back in Kittery. He had really wanted to stop at Henry VIII for a sandwich, but they were closed. One could spend all day there just reading the corny puns in the menu before diving into one of their delicious little offerings.

Oh well, too late to be worrying about that. Advanced planning and being nice to his digestive tract were not qualities for which Liam was well known. Suffer, he would, for this mistake later in the day and it was doubtful that he would learn from the experience. Stuffing the unfinished bag of offal into his pouch, he removed his water bottle and took a long draw of the cool liquid. It didn't so much remove the flavor from his mouth as it did swirl it around to make sure that all of his taste buds had a chance to savor the sticky mush, but it couldn't hurt. Zipping the bag back up, he hoisted it to his shoulders, reminded himself that he was in fact wearing big boy pants and could do this, and stepped forward toward the cave.

Boulders, shattered tree trunks, charred dirt littered the once open and spacious mouth to the cave. On his first visit two years ago, the opening was visually blocked from the outside by a landslide of materials from the hillside above but was wide open and easy to navigate once one made it past the outer wall. He could remember scrambling up through the beaver's dam-like structure simply to get a better view of where the birds were flying in and out of, only to be amazed by the discovery lying just beyond his initial view. If it hadn't been for the joyful dive bombing of those wee avians while he was hiking along, he probably would have missed then entrance and never ventured inside.

Gosh, that would have been nice.

Now, though, the place was a freakin' mess. What had once been a fairly clean rock and well-packed dirt floor during his earlier inspection was now a rubble field of random detritus. Walking along the path just before the winding cave dove into the bowels of the mountain, he ran his hand along the rocky wall. His fingertips came back black and dusty, scraping up remnants of the charring from the inferno cast within the opening from the ill-targeted missile strike during the pilot's encounter with the beast. Little had been released formally regarding the incident, but word-of-mouth had spread like wildfire once the pilot had been rescued and debriefed back at base. During the fight (if that's what one could even pretend to call it) the man had taken what would have been a clean kill shot on anything other than a dragon. Launching a sidewinder missile at the winged beast, the pilot missed the intended target and sent the envoy of destruction straight down the mouth of the cavern. It should have been the end of things, but as Liam and many others had found out the hard way, that dragon was no easy prey.

Wiping his hand on the leg of his pants, he grimaced at the streaks of ash and soot left behind. While he was wearing an older pair of pants, he didn't relish trying to wash all this crap out later tonight when he got back home. Dropping down on one knee, he looked side to side, quickly scanning the floor before him. Liam inspected a smattering of debris littering the rough, craggy surface of the naturally formed cave. Some items jumped to the fore of his mind immediately as recognizable bits from long-known sources while many others eluded his recognition.

Rising to his feet, Liam grabbed a stick from the side of the pathway and poked at the ground. Carefully raking through the mess, he found blasted chunks of rock, small animal bones, and heaps of unidentifiable charred remains of some organic matter. While he had never seen the results from a rocket detonation in real life, the scene before him looked just like anything he'd seen in a Michael Bay movie.

Pulling his headlamp from the backpack, he slipped it over his short brown hair and nestled it into place on his forehead. Rapidly cycling through the button options, he settled on the bright white long beam setting and continued down the path. Scanning back and forth as he walked, he looked in vain for anything of interest as he worked his way deeper into the mountainside. Whether blown to bits in the blast or stolen by previous adventurers, he was beginning to think that this whole trip was a waste of time.

Reaching for his temple, he pressed hard against the throbbing vein threatening to burst forth from his head. While he was fully aware of his growing anxiety as he had approached the cave entrance earlier this morning, he hadn't realized until then just how it was taking a toll on him physically. It was one thing to suffer mentally and emotionally from forcing oneself back to a dark place of his formative years, but he hadn't imagined the actual pain that he'd experience.

Taking a swig of water, he made himself breathe in through his nose and out through his mouth. It was an old trick that his mom had taught him when he was a child to overcome the nausea that plagued him regularly. He still doubted that it really had much impact on his gut, but the brief focus which he had to use to breathe like this probably had some net benefit on his psyche as he tried to actively not think about things to not think about. His brain was a wonderfully insane place to be.

Rounding a long meandering corner as he continued his way down the path, he came to the first of two obvious points of interest: the Armory.

Well, it obviously didn't have a real name, at least that he knew of, but that was how he had thought about this alcove since his last visit.

From what he could recall, there was a hoard of weapons—both fixed blade and more reasonably modern firearms; various forms of armor from different cultures; as well as a venerable cavalcade of random trinkets and accessories which one would find on men-of-arms throughout the past centuries. Liam could remember hiding behind a great bronze tower shield when the beast had rallied past him on its quest to end his life, only surviving because of the sheer size of the immense trophy.

Turning his head side to side in a vain attempt to cast more light about the wall where the entrance had once been, Liam sighed. To say he was dismayed would have been an understatement. While the second spot on this little journey of his was anticipated to be the more lucrative of his venture, he had hyped up this stop to be the absolute coolest and couldn't wait to find it again. He was almost ashamed to admit how bummed out he was to not get a chance to discover and salvage the breadth of historical pieces waiting for him within that offshoot of the cave. But from what he could see, there was literally no way in there without blasting the damn thing with dynamite.

Getting down on his hands and knees, he scurried across the floor, looking in and out of every available nook and cranny within the pile of boulders filling the former passage to his would-be treasure. Even with some of the biggest cracks being wide enough to slip his hand into, the average gaps between the rocks were paper thin. Not a single streak of light, puff of breeze, or crawling insect emerged from behind the wall of stone. As far as he was concerned, Liam was never getting through.

"Freakin' missile!" he groaned, kicking a rock into the darkness.

With slumped shoulders, he turned from the rubble and head down the length of the cave. The echoing clacks and cracks of the rocked propelled from the tip of his frustrated foot ricochetted from wall to wall, bombarding his ears with the high pitched record of its journey. Normally, it would have probably bounced once or twice and that would be the end of it... but it kept going.

Crack!

Clang!

Bang!

...

Splash.

Liam froze. He knew that he was tired and a little worked up, and that his senses may not be as acute as they would normally... but he knew the sound of a rock splashing into water when he heard it. Standing absolutely still, he paused for a moment longer, eagerly awaiting a further conclusion to this new auditory mystery. Sure enough, he heard more sounds.

A gentle babble of water meandering in and out, and up and over well-worn stones deep within the earth. The soothing whistle of water whirling through an errant vortex formed between a group of rocks. The splashing of rogue waves darting over rocks in their way, pushing and sloshing through the unexpected turbulence of stones blocking their journey.

Breaking into a run, Liam shot down the path, racing into the darkness as fast as his feet could take him. Not one to typically be this reckless, but the pure excitement of actually finding something on this trip after his disappointment with the Armory drove him beyond reason. Liam launched from one step to another, expertly navigating the floor of the cavern despite the low light. He hurdled over small boulders and dashed around bigger obstacles, quickly bringing himself closer to the end.

With the imagined glitter of the pile of gold shining in his eyes, he broke around what should have been the last bend in the tunnel. He poured on the speed, driven by the increasing volume of the subterranean stream echoing throughout the surrounding stone. Following the bouncing circle of light playing across wall, he gently leaned his weight to the right as he tracked the course of the path up ahead. Leaping over a small crack in the stone floor, he deftly landed on the other side and was about to do so again when he felt his foot slide out from under him.

Slamming his back into the rock below, he barely had time to recognize the view of the floor and walls around him change to the ceiling, then an upside down look at the path behind him, and the dark waters below. Liam tumbled down through the crevasse, desperately throwing his hands out into the inky blank air beyond looking to grab onto anything and everything within his grasp. Fire shot up his leg as his knee cracked into something hard and unforgiving. He instinctively pulled his left hand up behind his head to dull the impact should that be next. His right hand outstretched, he raked his fingers across the rough stone wall of the opening, crying out with pained joy as they ultimately found purchase on an outcropping.

His fall momentarily arrested, his momentary joy was quickly erased by the feeling of blood oozing from his palm. The sharp edge of the stone was cutting into his flesh, threatening to send him from the ledge and into the icy waters below. Carefully squirming one finger after another, he slowly adjusted his one-handed grip. Confident in his hold, he reached out with his left arm, swinging it through the air until it came to land on what felt like the same jutting rock. Nearing the point of hyperventilation, Liam stared ahead at the off-white circle of light blasting the granite face of the rift carved into the mountain cave. He tried to focus on the spot, consciously thinking of each rapid breath entering and exiting his overworked lungs, struggling to slow their pace. His heart hammered the inside of his chest, threatening to burst forth like a baby xenomorph, covering the rocky face of the ledge in his visceral essence.

Closing his eyes, he held on and waited. He held onto the rock. He held on to the sounds of the cave around him. He held on to the darkness threatening to surround and suffocate him. He absorbed the fear and anxiety threatening to course through his bloodstream, and pushed back. Pushing off from the rock with his knees, he thrust his feet forward and found purchase. With four points of contact on the rock face, he found the clarity that he needed and forced the calm determination that he knew himself to be capable of through his veins. His heart rate slowed. His hyperventilation subsiding, he took long, slow deep breaths from the cool air around him, and for the first time since entering the cavern, he appreciated being here.

Breathing slowly, he opened his eyes and looked around. It was time to get out of here before he slipped again. It would have been great to find some of that gold, but it wasn't worth losing his life to cold, dank dragon-scented hole in the ground. Letting the light play across the smooth, rolling surface of the cliff face, Liam could see several pieces jutting out here and there. If he was creative in how he grabbed onto them and strategized his path upward, he just might make it.

Reaching out, he easily got his hand on the first one. Confident in his hold, he swung his feet up and over, landing them harshly on the rubble-laden surface. The sole of his boot slipped and skidded, but finally found purchase toward the end of the feature. He continued on like this for several meters across the face, making his way mostly laterally across the surface, but gained a little elevation with each passing foot crossover. Stretching his arm out, he grabbed onto a sharp rock up ahead of him, squeezing the stone tightly between his aching fingers as he fought the never ending pull of gravity below.

And that was when he saw it.

Just out of the corner of his eye, about the length of his body away and to the right, the glimmer of metal reflected his headlamp's light back into his eye. Whether it was the magical twinkle of the light shining in this otherworldly cave that shouldn't exist in a normal, non-dragon world; the dream of newfound riches; or just the love of finding something new and shiny Liam was entranced. He couldn't look away. The more he stared, the more that he realized that it wasn't just a piece of metal, but a scattered collection of gold coins half buried in the debris on another outcropping.

Without consideration for his bodily health or any semblance of what would be required for success, Liam lunged outward. All that he could see, let alone remotely think about at that moment, was scooping up as much of the gold in one shot and showering himself in a luxurious and numismatically thrilling cascade of gleaming coins.

Each coin was probably worth at least two-grand alone and who knows how many (if any) of them were historically significant. And the fact that they had come from a legitimate dragon horde? Heck, beat-up silver coins claiming to be from a pirate vessel sunk in the Caribbean would fetch four to five times their normal value just for the cool factor.

His eyes zeroed in on the glittering target. Liam completely lost sight of what should have been his primary goal all along: grabbing onto the next handhold.

Flying through the air, he shot out past where he should have stuck a safe landing and continued onward toward the gold. His forearms slammed into the rock face, and he frantically struggled to find something to grab. He raked his fingers across the stone, just barely catching on as his fingernails scraped across the slick wall. Several of the coins bounced away as his body bashed into the rock, and he cried out in anguish as they disappeared into the murky dark below.

Gripping the stone with his left hand and relying on his feet to hold his weight on some tiny nubs below, he lunged once more. His arm stretched painfully beyond where its muscles and ligaments dared to go, and shot out toward the remaining gold coins. Liam felt his fingertips grace a few of them. He clutched at them, desperate to get something out of this insane move and make the pain and peril worthwhile. The coins bounced from his grasp, flying up and out away from the small shelf and his flailing fingers. His empty hand swatted at the cloud of precious metals exploding from their hiding place, and without a single thought for the future or his wellbeing, he reached out with his left hand and flew off into the dark void.

By the time that Liam realized what was happening, he was already held in gravity's grasp and screaming as his whole body fell downward. In the bleak moment of panic, time slowed down for the young man as he reflected on the decisions that had led him to this stupid situation. Greed; the desire to prove to others, and himself, that he really came face to face with this dragon and barely escaped with his life; the desire to have some financial benefit to help pay for the crap that he's had to deal with since this all began. Heck, it could all be whittled down to his desire to go for a hike one day several years back and play in a pool of cool water with the fish. If he had never seen those friggin' birds flying in and out of the hillside, he never would have ventured down here and awoken the slumbering beast within.

And so, he fell. His mind returned to the now and he quickly embraced the moment and resigned himself to his fate. He would fall into the murky darkness below, probably injure himself on the rocks below and, if he didn't die on impact, would most likely drown as his broken body succumbed to the relentless pounding of the underground stream. Closing his eyes, he felt himself begin the final plummet toward the icy water below...

Fire tearing through every bone and muscle from his shoulder to his hand, Liam felt himself jerk to a halt. He swung from an unknown force above him, slamming into the wall as physics took hold of his mass and fought his mystery rescuer. Wrenching his head up and around the rock jutting from beside him, he looked up to see a hand emerging from the surrounding shadows clamped around his wrist. The knuckles were white as the person struggled with all their might to hold on to him and arrest his descent.

Swinging his free hand up and over, Liam swatted at the rock, feeling around until he found a small nub to hold on to. Bracing his legs below him, he was finally able to get all of his limbs in some semblance of control and support himself.

"Here!" a voice rang from the murky dark above him. Liam tried to move his head in the direction of the words but couldn't locate the speaker. "Grab onto this!"

A length of green and yellow braided dynamic rope fluttered past him, whipping past his body and within arm's reach. The end disappeared below his feet, but the line stayed put, calling out to him. Liam grabbed the rope and pulled it close to him. He was about to simply hold on and try to climb but thought better of it. His muscles burned and his mind wasn't operating at full capacity. Doubt crept into his consciousness with each progressive thought, threatening to figuratively, and literally, throw him from this cliff.

Readjusting the fingers on his left hand, he quickly thought back to his years of climbing training and remembered the Alpine Butterfly. It wasn't glamorous and wouldn't be good for a long term haul, but it would help him get up to the top. With well-practiced hands and his memory coming through for him in this dire moment of need, he deftly maneuvered the rope in his one hand and rapidly fashioned the loop. If he didn't tie it correctly, it could slip and tighten up on him, so he didn't want to slide his arm into it, but the loop of rope would work well as a short-term handle. Taking the loop into his right, he gave it a test tug and was satisfied to see it taut.

"On belay?" he yelled up into the dimly lit space above.

Liam couldn't see much more than the movement of rope and limbs, but between his headlamp flickering around and the other lights playing across the ceiling of the cave beyond, he estimated that there must be at least three other people up there.

"Heh, what a nerd," the mystery voice said, the laughter barely concealed. "Hold on; we'll pull you up."

Brushing the thinly veiled insult aside, Liam held onto the rope with both hands and spread his feet apart on the stone wall. As the rope began to pull him up, he kept himself away from the rock by gently bouncing along on the balls of his feet. He didn't want to sway and jeopardize the grip of the person pulling him up, but he didn't want to get dragged along the surface, either.

A moment later, he found himself emerging from above the smooth surface of the cave proper and came face-to-face with his rescuers. The shining lights from their headlamps obscured his vision and he couldn't see who they were. But they had helped him out of a jam thanks to their incredibly convenient timing... of being right where and when he needed them at a remote cave in The-Middle-of-Nowhere, Maine. Too tired to think on it anymore, he filed that away for later. Worrying about that was a Tomorrow-Liam problem.

A hand reached out and he gratefully took hold of it. The man who had originally grabbed his hand down below was climbing up beside him on an adjacent rope, preparing to grab onto awaiting climbers above. The two men rounded the edge of the cliff as the others helped to pull each one up. Allowing himself to be hoisted up and over by hand and rope, Liam popped back onto flat ground for a change. He tried to talk but needed a moment. Resting his hands on his knees, he stayed bent over for a moment, then slowly stretched upward, leaning back against the wall of the cave. The woman who helped him up reached out quickly and grabbed his shoulders, steadying him before he could fall over once more.

"Woah," Liam managed in between breaths. "Thanks a lot, guys. I thought that I was a goner back there. If you hadn't arrived when you did, I don't know what would have happened."

The three newcomers stared back at him. One of the men gently nudged the woman in the side, who quickly straightened up. "Oh, yes, of course! What's, ah, a good fellow-climber to do, right?"

The three looked to Liam, then back to each other.

"Yeah, man, you'd do the same for us," the second man said.

The third man, the one who climbed up alongside Liam, continued to look on. Liam wasn't sure to make of him, but he knew when he was being sized up. Was the guy looking to fight him? Was he judging him for the fall and not being able to save himself? Because if he was, Liam only needed a few more minutes and, well, surely would have gotten up out of that ravine on his own if he really had to... right?

Liam, finally able to catch his breath and stand up without the support of the rock wall, straightened upward, stretching out side-to-side in a vain attempt to bring his muscles back to life. He wasn't sure yet just what exactly he had done to his body during this little debacle, but new knew for certain that he would feel it tomorrow. Brushing a few streaks of crushed stone dust from his shirt, he tried to smooth out his clothes and seem presentable to the other, clearly better skilled climbers.

"So, what brings you all out here on this fine day to go cave falling?" Liam said, trying to break the tension.

The woman chuckled. "We, uh, heard about that fighter jet that had an accident a while back," she started, motioning toward the beginning of the cave. "It was all pretty hush hush from where we're from, so we wanted to come and check it out."

Liam's ears perked up at the mention of the jet. *Yeah, an accident, alright,* he thought. *An accidental run-in with a flamethrower mounted on a pair of scaley wings.*

"Yeah, that was weird, huh?" he managed, struggling to think of something to say without playing his cards. "Where did you drive in from?"

"Southish," the glaring man said. His face was obscured in the dark, but Liam could make out a hint of a scowl as he looked down at him.

"Hey!" the woman chimed in. "Why don't we head back outside and get some fresh air, huh? You need a drink? I got a thermos in my pack with some nice cool water."

"Yeah, sure," Liam said, following her lead. He looked back over his shoulder as the four walked back up the path. His heart sank into his stomach as he watched the end of the cave disappear into the darkness. This whole trip had been a waste, and he had almost died in the process with nothing to show for it.

Ten minutes later, after getting that promised drink while being hastily shooed along the cave and away from the entrance, Liam was back at the truck. He still didn't know what to make of that trio. Sure, they had saved his sorry butt back there and had been nice enough about getting him back on his feet and into sunlight again, but there was a weird vibe about all of it. It was like they knew something that he didn't and wanted him out of there.

Of course, he knew something that they didn't too, right?

Sliding across the red fabric of the bench seat in his aging F150, he felt something digging into the right side of his thigh. Reaching down, he felt along the length of his shorts, searching for whatever sliver or chuck of rock must have gotten stuck in the fabric and was threatening his nervous system with tiny pokes. Slipping his hand into the cargo pocket, his fingers crept along the length and width, struggling to come up with anything of note which may explain the sensation.

And then, he felt it. A thin, round object was stuck in the inner fold where the pocket is sewed into the pant leg. His thumb slide across the face and he could feel gentle ridges and slopes, like the carved head of a person. As he removed it from his pocket and held it before him, a golden glow reflected off its surface from the late afternoon sun, highlighting his smile.

"Status report," a voice commanded from the speaker on the two-way radio clipped to the woman's backpack. The voice of Lady Lucy was one inspired fear and respect from their group, depending on your own behavior and recent accomplishments. While she had been pretty easy going lately, enough of the Order of Draco knew of her dark past and what she had done to get to her place in the shadows to tread lightly.

"Ma'am," the woman began, holding down the call button, "we followed the Target and found the destination, as anticipated. Target led us directly to both objectives prior to having a minor accident."

"An accident? Is everyone alright?"

"Yes, ma'am," she continued. "Our team provided assistance after he fell down an unanticipated fissure within the cave system. The initial scans didn't pick it up and we assume that it was caused by the missile strike detailed in the pilot's report."

"Understood," Lady Luce responded. "Where is the target now?"

"We helped him along and he has returned to his personal vehicle. We have Satellite 5 tracking his position now. As far as we could tell, he didn't know us or why we were there."

"Good," the woman in Worcester said, her voice growing more serious. "And the objectives?"

"Objective 1 is behind a wall of caved in rock, also presumably from the explosion, but our scans show the items to be intact. Operatives 2 and 3 are excavating as we speak and should have news within six hours. The status of Objective 2 is unknown for now, but we will descend into the fissure and perform visual and sensory scans to locate the gold. Operative 3 claims to have seen something akin to golden coins on a ledge during the initial descent, but they were possibly lost during rescue of the Target."

"Understood," the voice said, trailing off into a long pause. Beads of sweat formed on the younger woman's forehead which didn't belong there in the cooler temperature of this part of Maine. "Good job, Operative 1. Continue your mission and report back in the morning. Lucy, out."

WORK RELEASE

Stepping off the bus and into the bright afternoon sunlight, Mal Akili breathed deeply of the cool New England air. The scents of evergreen and deciduous trees, flowers, and a nearby river intermingled within his nostrils, bringing back an influx of old, happy memories. This was the first taste of freedom that he'd had in almost two years, and he was going to enjoy every possible moment of it. Looking up, he stared at the blue sky above his head and just marveled at it. Granted, it didn't look any different than the view he had seen from behind the tall prison walls, but it just felt better for some reason. He could have stood there all day just soaking it all in if it weren't for the butt of the rifle jabbing him from behind.

Wincing from the hit, he looked over his shoulder and shot the guard a menacing looking. He couldn't really do anything to the man, he was still restrained by the shackles around his wrists and ankles, but he couldn't let the offense go without a dirty look. Seeing the stern glare solidified upon the other man's face, Mal let it slide and decided to move onward. He was about to start a new chapter in his life and didn't want to blow his chances. If he stuck to the plan, kept his mouth shut and his nose down, he could ride out his contract and be completely free within five years. Well, at least that's what they had told him.

Walking in a sloppily straight column along with the other prisoners, he looked around as they made their way through what appeared to be the back entrance to wherever they were going. Nondescript and seemingly devoid of signs or advertising, the entrance was merely a door burrowed into the side of a hill with no known purpose. As they passed through the armored double doors, his new world jumped into view.

Gazing around at his surroundings, he couldn't believe the things that he was seeing. Their walk took them by a vast series of rooms and sub-divisions. Their guards kept yelling at them to stare ahead, but from what he could see during a few surreptitious glimpses, there was a large training arena for the creatures he had heard about, testing labs, research rooms, and an expansive library. The fact that these people took the time to collect and curate physical paper books in this day and age deeply impressed him. Most similar facilities had all but switched to digital-only media to save on money and floor space. These people were either well-funded, interested in older arcane information, or probably both. The rich folk always liked to collect weird things.

Venturing further into the complex, the small group finally came to the prison barracks. He had expected their housing to be some typical jail building set within a large ring of barbed wire fencing. But not here. From what he could tell given their little tour, the entire jail was underground and buried deep within a well-protected compound. Either they trusted the prisoners not to run or they knew that they wouldn't get far.

"This deal is getting better by the minute," he whispered to himself, looking around for other ways to sneak out or hide as they progressed.

Later that night as he sat alone on the bed of his single medium-security room, he turned and laid his head back onto the pillow. Sinking into the firm, yet delicately soft cotton stuffing, (which was more glamorous than anything he had seen in years) he stared up at the concrete ceiling and felt his eyes begin to close. As he drifted off to sleep, his brain travelled back in time to his younger self...

He was 26 and in graduate school. After completing his undergrad degree at UC Berkley, focusing on vertebrate zoology, he had made his way out to the east coast to Harvard. He adored the northeast and reveled in the unusual climate and the hardy animals it produced. While at Harvard, he used his time to further explore the world of reptiles, ultimately deciding to concentrate in herpetology. He had even been fortunate enough to conduct multiple woodland experiments out in Central Mass, namely at their dedicated research forest in Petersham. After saving a bit of money and petitioning for support with his advisor, he was able to secure a grant to perform a study abroad trip to Costa Rica. Now, back at Berkley, he was about to begin his doctoral candidacy while interning at the San Diego Zoo.

He was ecstatic to finally get his hands on some real projects with actual scientific merit and begin contributing to his field. He had spent far too long stuck in labs and dark corners of the library and needed to stretch his wings. Mal knew that he had the academic smarts, the drive, and the work ethic to make a difference in the world. He just needed the chance to prove himself. Thanks to a stunning letter of recommendation from his thesis advisor at Harvard and four years of stellar grades, he managed to secure himself a place in the reptile wing of the zoo and would be working predominantly with the Komodo dragons. He had spent a large portion of his graduate work thus far researching different species of the larger reptile families, and to finally make it to a position such as this was a tremendous honor for him.

Unfortunately, it was all going to cost him a small fortune, of which he did not have. While he had been extremely lucky to garner sufficient funding for his undergrad program through various loans, grants, and work study programs, he had been forced to take out numerous additional private loans to complete his master's degree. He landed a highly sought-after research assistant role with his advisor and provided TA support to a few courses, but it just wasn't enough to make ends meet. He ended up taking out loan after loan after loan after painful and never-ending loan to supplement his RA stipend, leaving him buried in debt for years to come. Even with his diligent saving and sending in what little extra he had each month, the interest payments were killing him and burying his financial future.

That is, until the other day when his friend had shown him a possible way out. A former roommate from several years back, the individual had been a finance major and spent his days buying and selling stocks for both personal and professional gain. Working as a stockbroker for a large firm while simultaneously building his own portfolio for retirement, the man knew the ins and outs of the market and could navigate it with impressive ease. Over beers one night at their favorite watering hole from their undergrad days, the friend had mentioned a plan that he had come up with to pool together funding from various investors to help build his own net worth while bringing everyone else along with him. He knew that Mal was looking to pay down his loans while supporting his work on his PhD and offered to bring him in on the ground floor. While the offer sounded too good to be true and a little confusing to Mal's ears, he needed the money and was beginning to get desperate. If he didn't come up with something soon, he knew that he'd spend a significant portion of his adult life paying off his loans and never reap the financial benefits of his hard work.

After carefully considering his friend's offer and battling the inner financial turmoil brewing within his head, he ultimately relented and agreed to buy into the deal with his buddy. And why wouldn't he? The arrangement was straightforward and guaranteed that his money would pay back dividends countless times over. All that he had to do was give his friend $10,000 in cash within a few weeks, send some emails around and follow-up with phone calls to their investors, and he'd be on the path to financial freedom. Asking around, he located a guy in town who specialized in high-interest cash loans with no questions asked, paid his share to the friend, and chipped in with the administrative work. Granted, he didn't get much sleep while still focusing on his doctoral research, but he knew that this was just a moment in time and would be over soon. The short term pain would pay out in the end. There was no way that this could go wrong…

Waking up in a cold sweat just as the morning light shone through his window, Mal remembered quite vividly just how wrong things had gone. It had been almost six years now, but the memories had been laser etched into his hippocampus and replayed themselves in excruciatingly accurate details every night in his nightmares. Between the plan turning out to be an elaborate Ponzi scheme orchestrated by his friend; the Feds investigating and lumping Mal in with his buddy; and convicting him on multiple counts of securities fraud; he had found himself a resident of the federal prison system within six months of joining in on the investment program. In the blink of an eye, he had thrown away a bright future in a prestigious career at the top of his field and all the financial security that he could dream of. All because he couldn't fathom how to pay back his tuition payments before retirement. Ah, the American Dream.

"What a moron," he mumbled to himself as he stepped out of the cell and into the hallway beyond. He was painfully aware that at the end of the day, this was sort of his own fault. He could have gone to school for a less demanding degree program with cheaper tuition. He could have gotten a second job to help pay down his student loans. He could have done a multitude of other arguably better options than to get caught up in a financial scheme that, looking back on it, he should have spotted as a scam from a mile away. He was smarter than that. Shoulda, woulda, coulda. It didn't matter much now.

Joining the ranks of the other inmates, they made their way to the shower rooms, then off to breakfast, and eventually down to the meeting room. Today was orientation day and they would be learning the ins and outs of their new jobs. He still had no clue as to what he was going to be doing here but had an inkling that it would pertain to herpetology in some shape or form. When he was previously approached at the prison, the woman he had spoken with had gone on and on about his previous experience, education, and interests in future research. She had never asked about his crimes, whether he was guilty or innocent, nor if he would ever get in trouble again. It was all very odd. For a person to speak with an inmate like this, you think that she would have been slightly concerned about his past or inclination towards danger. If he didn't know any better, he'd swear that he was on the outside again simply sitting down for an informal job interview for anything besides being trapped in a concrete and steel cell.

Shuffling through the procession of disgruntled yawning prisoners, he was ultimately led to a room down the hall beyond a thick steel door. Looking around as he passed through the portal and into the room beyond, he paused midstride and quickly took in the sight of a table, four chairs, and very little else. The room was cold. And not just cold in temperature, but cold feeling. It felt as if people who entered this room left different people... if they left at all.

Mal could feel the blood pressure spiking within his body, sending pulsing waves of distress up and down his spine. His arms and legs tingled as arteries were flush with hot blood and adrenaline. Every ounce of his being told him to flee the room and get out of there. Not that he could have. As he'd learned in the past twenty-four hours, this place, while giving the illusion of a medium security prison, had only one real exit and it wasn't through the front door.

And during the night... he had heard things.

Feeling a shove from behind, he was jolted from mental wanderings and snapped back to the moment. He took the hint and continued forward, passing through the doorway. Unarmed and surrounded from all sides, there was little else that he could do. If they said, *jump*; he asked, *how high*? This was his life now.

The guard behind him firmly assisted his forward motion and ordered him to stand before the table. Looking down to his feet, he noticed an X painted onto the tile floor. The guard quickly relocated and stood in the back corner by the door through which they had just entered, rigidly standing at attention. From observing their behavior, he got the feeling that they didn't have much more freedom than he did.

The room was relatively small with only enough space for the aforementioned items, a mirrored surface on the back wall, and the smooth flooring on which he was standing. An unassuming closed door resided on the wall to Mal's left, his only way out of the chamber aside from the defended portal at his back. He stared at the door, wondering when it would open and who, or what, would come marching through. The anticipation alone was most likely worse than anything which could reasonably come through the small entryway, but that didn't stop him from imagining the worst.

After a few minutes of anxious waiting, and several nervous glances back at his assigned overseer, the door finally opened to reveal four people quickly walking through and moving to their chairs. Each took a seat in what felt like a well-rehearsed ritual. As the quartet settled into their respective chairs, they squared up some papers, skimmed through notes, and whispered back and forth with one another. They seemed to almost not notice his presence, save for the middle-aged woman on the far end. Throughout a series of hushed comments exchanged with the man to her side, she had kept her eyes trained upon Mal.

Looking back to her, having long ago decided to ignore the other three as they apparently had decided likewise with him, he got the feeling that she wasn't afraid of him. That sense was new to him. He had long felt feared and avoidable once the stigma of *criminal* had been placed upon him years ago. When she noticed that he had latched onto this and kept an eye on her, her eyes darted to a corner of the room. Watching her, he could see that she was trying to look anywhere but at him, but every few moments, her eyes would just barely look his way again. As the game continued, he began to realize what was really going on; she was sizing him up. It was as if she wanted to appear to merely consider him as an asset to utilize and not really a person. But he could tell that she was failing to do so. She may be calculating, but she wasn't without a heart.

He'd need to file that away, he thought. Perhaps he could play into her emotions later. Yet, as soon as he pondered this notion, his stomach roiled in disgust. This wasn't him. He wasn't some hardened criminal who would shoot his way out of here. He was a goddamn scientist and just wanted to do his job. What had happened to him?

The thought, though momentarily buoying his spirits, now plummeted his morale into the proverbial ground. He was a prisoner and would continue to be so until he had served his sentence in full and repaid his debt to society... a society that would never look at him the same way so for as long as he had a criminal history pop up in his background search. He might get out of here someday, but only when they were through with him and had gotten what they needed.

Without moving his head, he scanned the occupants of the table with his eyes and took in every detail available to him. What they were wearing, hair styles, writing stationery and computer equipment carried in, and their level of concern for his observations, were all filed away for future use. He hadn't been locked away from society for six years without learning a few tricks. Which still felt a little bizarre to him when he thought about it. He had been a strait-laced, honorable citizen on the outside. Now he was ready to take advantage of another person's mistakes or temporary lapse in judgement if it meant freedom for him.

Hearing their conversations begin to wan and the volume in the room drop as they resumed their discussion, Mal straightened up and stood at attention. From what he could tell, these were either military officers or closely connected in some form, so he figured that it couldn't hurt to play into their customs. Looking straight ahead and waiting for them to speak first, he couldn't help but notice that the woman on the far left was watching him again, and this time, she was smiling.

"Good morning, Mr. Akili," the woman finally said, hushing the rest of her group with a subtle hand motion. "My name is Dr. Anastasio," she began, a hand pointing to her chest. "And this is Darmond, Warden Norton, and Mr. Robbins."

Mal watched as the man called Darmond rose from his seat in a humble indication of himself and quickly sat back down. The warden just glared back at him, and the man known as Mr. Robbins offered a small wave. He nodded back to each one in turn.

"Thank you for joining us this morning. Have you enjoyed your stay so far at our… um… facility?" Dr. Anastasio asked.

A laugh blurted out through Mal's tightly pursed lips. He hadn't meant to drop his defenses so easily and let it slip, but it was hard not to. The question was either hilariously tone deaf or the woman was amazingly callused to his predicament.

"Oh, yes," Mal began, "very much so. I'm lined up to get a massage this afternoon, and me and the boys are playing soccer later tonight after our three-course supper."

The man identified as Darmond blurted out a poorly disguised laugh, clearly incapable of playing this covert, shadow ops game that the others were engaged in. Mal could see the faintest hint of a smirk creep across the woman's face. Looking to the right, he saw that the warden and the suit at the end of the table were not amused.

"That's great to hear. I hope that you enjoy it," Dr. Anastasio commented, moving on without a hiccup. "As we discussed in our last meeting a few months back, this… erm… property, is a research facility that is designed to study, nurture, and train a special breed of creatures that are critical to the operational needs of our organization. In addition to the personnel and equipment that I'm sure you've noticed on your way in here so far, we are always on the lookout for bright, enthusiastic people to join our team and assist in our experimental work.

"You indicated during our last discussion that our activities and mission statement were of interest to you and that you'd be inclined to learn more about our projects and help us in any way possible. Is that still the case?"

Mal couldn't hold back his excitement. This sounded even cooler than he had originally been told. "Of course," he said. "It would be my honor."

"Good," she said, motioning to him. "Why don't you have a seat?"

The guard by the door slid a metal folding chair over to where he stood and placed it just behind his knees. Mal, still bearing the set of handcuffs and ankle shackles, carefully bent, and sat down on the cold chair.

"Now, why don't you tell us a little more about yourself," the doctor said.

Clearing his throat, Mal dove into his academic background up to this point, his goals for future study, and his interests, both within and outside of the scholarly circles. He was hesitant at first, not fully sure of what they really wanted with him and if giving up personal information voluntarily could hurt or help him, but his inhibitions slowly dissipated as he worked his way through each subsequent thought. Mal told them about his hobbies (albeit a small number of them beyond the scope of reptile and animal studies) and how he thought that he could better purpose his skills and experience in the outside world beyond the prison walls.

Watching their faces as his story progressed, he could sense that they wanted more. His tale of past experiences and achievements was cursory at best and abysmally dry at worst. Decided to spice things up a little, he took the time to outline his well-meaning activities which led to his arrest and eventual prison time. Trying to read their faces as he continued to speak, he could see an understanding nod come from the man named Darmond, and something of a smile from the woman on the left. The two dullards on the right, as expected, were emotionless sacks of meat wasting oxygen in the room. What he wouldn't give to get these shackles off and dive back into some real science with the former two and put this drudgery behind him. A guy like him didn't belong in jail! Hell, he should be running this place by now.

Putting the finishing touches on the answer to the last of his questions, a rather dry administrative question about past behavior in his previous facility and how he would behave at this new one, Mal took a deep breath and adjusted his position within the chair. His spine straightened and he subconsciously adjusted his feet, moving them from a crooked angle where he would have lost circulation to his extremities had he remained there much longer. The hard edge of the cheap steel chair was digging into the underside of his legs, threatening future pain and discomfort to any unwilling test subjects who failed to move around from time to time.

Looking from face to face, he tried to gauge their reactions to his testimony. He tried to see how emotionally connected they were to his side of the story, to his version of the accounts and possible sympathize with the mistakes that he had made and why. He hoped beyond hope that they would see that he was just a brilliant man trying to make his mark in the world and that he had gambled on a get-rich-quick scheme that backfired on him. Surely, they must see that the ends would justify the means and that he could make great strides within their corner of the academic community were he to be released and given his freedom to go back to work. His pulse rushing, he found his breath shorten and come in quicker puffs and gasps. The suspense was going to kill him before this blasted prison would and he needed to know right here and now what they were going to decide.

He didn't have to wait for long.

Dr. Anastasio cleared her throat, leaning forward to look down the length of the table at each of her colleagues. Her eyes subtly shifted from face to face, quickly sealing the deal with a trio of rapid-fire nods. She turned back toward Mal.

"Thank you, Mr. Akili," the doctor said, her voice flat.

Gone was the guarded yet cheerful tone from earlier in the meeting. Mal wasn't sure what had just changed, but the positive head nods was promising at least... right?

"We appreciate your time here this morning and being afforded the chance to learn more about you and your background, thus far," she continued. "Our team believes that you and your well-earned qualifications would be highly beneficial to the goals and personnel of our program. If you're still interested, we have an open position for you here within this facility for which you'd be perfect. What do you think?"

Mal beamed. After years of hard work, setbacks, dumb decisions, and time behind bars desperately trying to pay back his debt to society and make his way back into the world, he had finally found his way out. This would change everything.

"That—that would be perfect," Mal stammered.

He wanted to say more, wanted to let them know that they

wouldn't regret it and that they could count on him. He wanted to make sure that they knew that this was the chance he was waiting for and wouldn't let them down. But the words were lost on him as the feelings welled up within his body. Mal had come in here trying to be a hardass and thinking that he could con his way out of whatever BS they would lob at him. But now that he stood before his would-be employers and they were now talking to him not as a prisoner, but almost as an equal, the hard edge previously buffering his skin from the outer world dissolved. Mal was no longer a criminal willing to do anything and everything that he needed to advance his personal agenda and excel within the cutthroat world of academic competition, but a willing and eager young man yearning for the chance to prove himself once more.

"Yes," he continued, summoning the emotional strength to continue. "Yes, it would be an honor. Thank you for the opportunity."

They returned the commentary and welcomed him to the team. None of them got up to approach him or shake his hands or anything, but he didn't think much of it. He was too caught up in the moment, and after all, he was still a convicted criminal and detainee within a prison, even if it were about as unorthodox of a prison as possible.

The guard from before approached him and escorted him from the room. They passed by another inmate being led into the room by a different jailor. As his guard unlocked his shackles, Mal shot a look to the prisoner. "I got in!" he mouthed to the other man. He had hoped for some sort of congratulatory reply, but only got a dirty look.

Whatever.

Later that night, as he sat down on his bunk to eat his supper, Mal could barely contain himself. The butterflies in his stomach churned and danced about, threatening to send back any food that he ate, but he couldn't help it. For the first time in years, he was elated beyond belief. He was eating a warm meal, which was quite better than even what he had eaten earlier in the day; he had a job lined up; and people were talking to him like a real person again. Nothing could stop him now.

"Mal, how are you doing?" Stacy looked through the four inch thick multilaminar armored glass. Seeing the smiling man give her a thumbs-up, she turned her attention back to the laptop before her. Making a few quick notes, she pressed the call button the microphone once more.

"This is test number forty-one," she continued. "I am Dr. Stacy Anastasio, joined by doctoral candidate Mal Akili. Mal is in the chamber with the test materials awaiting the subject and will be performing all physical activities within the scope of the test procedure. Cameras are rolling."

She paused, consulting her screen once more. Taking her finger off the call button, she sat back in her chair. Looking to the aides beside her, she grinned. "This could be the one."

Leaning forward, she pressed a button on a different radio. "Dar, are you in position?"

"Yes, ma'am," he replied. "Subject is ready and hungry. This will be as good of an indicator as we'll get if this works."

"Understood," she said. "Standby."

"Mal," she said, pressing the first button. "Prepare for subject introduction. Remain with the nutrient offerings and observe the subject. Remain calm and record everything that you can observe."

"You got it!" he yelled. His voice blared through the speakers within the bunker. The multitude of omnidirectional microphones strategically placed around the test chamber were able to hear every scrape, slurp, and bone crunch that occurred within the four heavily fortified walls. "I mean, yes. Yes, ma'am."

"Good. Standby." Picking up the second radio she said, "Dar, please proceed."

At Stacy's command, Dar engaged the door locks on the cage and raised the blast door up and into the steel reinforced concrete ceiling of the holding chamber. He watched in awe as the black creature, about the size of a large horse at this point, passed by his viewing portal. The creature sniffed at the glass, and he wasn't sure, but it appeared that the thing glared at him. From what the engineers had said, the glass was supposed to be a one-way viewing portal, but that didn't help the sinking feeling that the thing knew he was there.

Watching from the control room bunker, Stacy watched in callused awe as the small black dragon lunged from the opening of its cage and dove toward the unsuspecting Mal Akili. The dragon tore into the unguarded flesh of the man, ripping muscle and bone from the frame of the human as spurts of thick red blood splattered the blast proof glass window. She subconsciously moved her hand to the audio controls to the right of her computer mouse, gently rolling the wheel to lower the volume on her speaker. The man's screams, sickly combining with the guttural shrieks of hungry rage from the winged creature, threatened to bore their way into her brain. She had learned several sessions back to be prepared for this moment.

"COME ON, Richard!" She moaned, staring through the glass at the young dragon. "You can't keep eating every single new scientist that we send in to work with you. Son of a bi—"

Dar's radio chimed in, interrupting her pending stream of obscenities which had become worse with each passing failed test. The crew had gotten used to it by now, despite her often elaborate descriptions of what the dragon could do to itself using what remaining body parts from the freshly murdered scientists and engineers were at its disposal.

"Ma'am," he radioed, his voice tenuous. "Uh, looks like that guy was a bust as well. What should I do?"

Raising her head from her hands, which she had been trying to support the growing weight of failure through, or at least apply enough pressure to stave off the growing migraine, Stacy stared through the glass at the beast beyond. She watched in disgust as the thing bent its long neck down to the body once more, picking at a rather bloody morsel of one of Mal's appendages.

"Unofficially, Dar," she began, taking a breath, "let the little jerk finish his meal. We paid for these prisoners to come in here, we might as well get something out of it. Officially, please move the subject back into the holding cell as soon as convenient and prepare for test number forty-two. Hopefully the Colonel will show a little restraint with this one and learn to stop eating all of our technical personnel."

THE NEWPORT NUISANCE

Jumping from the seats, the four friends quickly hustled their bikes over to the side of the unassuming house on Drury Lane. Wheeling them around to a recently installed rack on the back corner, out of eyesight from the road, they parked the bikes and ran up the steps to the front door. Zoe, the de facto leader of their little quartet, reached out to the hidden button in the side of the door and gently pushed it. Unless you knew where to look, it was almost impossible to find. Almost as well hidden as the small camera looking down at them through the tinted windows on each side of the door.

Stepping back, she motioned for the rest of the crew to stand still and wait. There were protocols to follow, and she knew them by heart. Zoe had been inducted into the Order a while back and was informally tasked with bringing her three friends up to speed. They had just recently been accepted and were still in their trial period, so they had to stay focused. She doubted that they could really do something bad enough to get kicked out, but then again, she had heard some pretty rough rumors about Lady Lucy and how strict she could be.

Just as she was beginning to get nervous that they wouldn't be allowed to enter, she heard the buzzer ring out from the electronic door lock. Smiling, she grabbed the knob and pushed in on the heavy wooden door. It was dark inside, but she could hear some commotion from further in the house. Waving her friends onward, she stepped over the threshold and into the gloom beyond.

"Woah, do you guys hear that?" Luca asked from just behind her. He was one of her braver friends and obviously not one to miss out on some fun. He started moving in right behind her, wanting to see this place for himself.

"Yeah," Zoe replied, quietly. "I think that someone's fighting back there. Why would they have let us in if there was danger?"

Luca looked back at her, equally puzzled.

"Wait, did you say someone's fighting?" A quiet voice quavered from the back of the group. "Let's get out of here!"

"Ease up, Giovanni!" Another girl said from the back of the group, gently elbowing him in the ribs and pushing past. "I'm sick of hearing Zoe's tales of this house without seeing it for ourselves. Let's get in there!"

Bristling at being called out, Giovanni gently shoved back at Stella and the two pushed their way inside. They barreled into Luca, and in turn, Zoe, sending the four companions hurtling to the dark floor of the entry way. Rising to their feet and dusting themselves off, they chuckled at the scenario. That is, until the sounds started again. Holding her finger to her lips, Zoe indicated that they should head straight toward the den in the back of the house.

Tiptoeing across the intricately woven rug covering the hardwood floor of the foyer, they started their way down the hallway and came to a sudden halt. A voice rang out through the still air, chilling their blood and freezing them in their tracks.

"BE GONE, FOUL DEMON!" The woman's voice bellowed out once more, the sounds echoing from the room beyond.

"I have journeyed over a thousand leagues in search of this treasure and will not turn back now for the likes of thee."

A loud roar rang out followed by growling and the jingle of metal on metal.

"What is that?" Stella whispered.

"It sounds like chains clanging," Giovanni pondered. "And maybe coins spilling?"

"And that roar... sounded almost like a dragon!" Luca whisper-shouted, clamping his hand over his mouth to quell his excitement. "I heard that you had some cool stuff down here, Zoe, but what exactly are you all up to?!"

The sound of wood skidding across the floor screeched out, and an old wooden chair came flying through the doorway up ahead, crashing into the wall to their right. Screams rang out from the room, followed by the distinct sounds of swords on armor.

"Yah! Get him!" an angry voice shouted out.

"Kill him!" another contributed.

Creeping toward the door, Zoe quietly made her way down the length of the hallway. She had just reached the point where it turned from painted drywall to an older construction stone wall, indicative of the true nature of the house. Turning to her friends, she flicked her head, motioning that she was going up to take a look. The friends, surprisingly, seemed inclined to follow. As one, they sprang toward the open door and crouched vertically along the height of the doorjamb, ready to peer beyond.

Gripping the stone trim of the door, they inched the sides of their heads past the last length of the wall and gazed upon the scene unfolding before them.

"I, Bonnie, the Warrior Princess of Clan Blackstone, the Golden One, Whisperer to Ducks, and Slayer of Smokers, will be your undoing!"

A woman clad in armor stood in front of a large, ornately carved wooden table. From what they could tell, she was in the position where the aforementioned chair, now crammed up against the wall to their backs, had once lived. The kids watched as she drew a sword from a scabbard on her belt, raised it to the ceiling, and thrust it out before her.

"Oh no!" cried Stella.

"Shh!" Zoe hissed. "We don't even know who she's attacking. Let's stay hidden until we know more.

Just then, a calm voice emanated from the far end of the table, breaking the silence.

"Bonnie thrusts her sword deep into the heart of Lord Fumus," a man spoke, his bass voice deep, penetrating your ears and enveloping you into his words. "We see the tip of her sword plunge into his ashen armor, pause for a moment, and burst through to the other side. As the tip of her blade emerges from his flaming cape, a shower of acidic blood erupts from his back, melting everything it touches."

"Woah!" A chorus of voices rang out from the shadows surrounding the dimly lit room. In the deathly quiet calm of the chamber, the sound of a resin polyhedron rolling across leather could be heard bouncing from surface to surface. Bonnie's fate had been cast.

"But as Bonnie pushes forward, driving the sword into Lord Fumus's chest until the hilt clangs into the polished front of his cuirass, a clawed hand reaches out from the darkness and tears into her shoulder."

"Ah!"

"Oh no!"

"Lord Fumus turns his face to meet Bonnie's, his eyes ablaze, and pulls her closer. His fiery breath roars into her face, scorching her eyebrows. Reaching out with his other hand, he grips her by the throat and raises her from the floor." Another roll of a die, this one seeming to bounce endlessly before settling on the final number. "Her crippled body flies across the dungeon, crashing into an ornate stone sculpture adjacent to the mausoleum entrance."

Bonnie stared down at the table, motionless. Very calmy, she reached next to her and retrieved a velvet bag.

"Roll a D20," the man's voice softly emerges from the darkness.

Bonnie's hand reached into the bag and produced a small object with twenty sides. Holding it up to one of the few lights in the room, she gazed into the semi-opaque surface, admiring the faint flecks of metallic silver embedded within the die. Lightly kissing the object, she whispered, "Don't fail me now."

The die dropped from her hand and fell into the opening of a wooden dice tower to the side of her character sheet. The clangs rang out from the structure, echoing around the room with each crashing descent from the top. Rolling out through the hole at the bottom, it came to rest at the landing below.

Bonnie gasped, staring down at the tiny chunk of resin. "A one," she whispered to the room.

The man's voice emerged from the far end of the dimly lit table.

"As Bonnie's body collides with the sculpture, her head slams against the edge of the base, killing her instantly. Her companions rush to her side, but their help is in vain. She is no more."

"What!?" Bonnie called out, staring at Conrad.

Conrad, one of the members of the Order of Draco, was also their resident game master for their tabletop role playing games. He was as professional as they come and tried to keep things fair but pulled no punches with the gamers. If you played a game under Conrad, victory was not a given. Until now, he had sat back out of the dim light, aiding in the general spookiness of the room. It wasn't until he and his best friend, Liam, leaned forward that the kids even knew they were in the room.

"Dude, you can't kill a PC!" Liam Tryggvison called out, stepping from the shadows toward the lit surface of the table. Liam, settling in to his now-relaxed role of dragon tamer after his many adventures of years past, was often found around the game table if there wasn't a dragon to care for.

"Hey!" Conrad shot back. "It's not my fault that she botched her saving throw. Besides, it was just a one-shot. We were only playing while we waited for the kids to get out of school."

"Speaking of which," Gena said from Conrad's side, flicking her chin toward the door. "Looks like we have some eavesdroppers."

Gena was second-in-command to Lucy, leader of the Worcester branch of the Order of Draco. While she wasn't as much of a nerd as her friends, she enjoyed hanging out with them during their games, especially if there was pizza to steal.

"We weren't dropping no eaves!" Zoe shot back to the amusement of all in the room. She felt at home with these giant nerds. "Sorry, we came in and heard fighting. We thought that someone was getting murdered back here."

"You could say that," the armored woman said, turning to face the four kids as they walked into the room. "Your buddy Conrad here was nice enough to let me borrow some of the less-than-historic pieces from the armory, enthusiastically pull me into an imaginary world of wonder and adventure, and ultimately guide me to my doom against Lord Fumus."

"You rolled the die, my dear," Conrad said, "and the die spoke. I am merely the storyteller."

Rolling her eyes at him, Bonnie turned back to Zoe and her friends. "My apologies if I scared you, young ones. We were playing through a new story which Conrad wrote and apparently, I now have my afternoon available. Which is perfect timing as you're now here. I have some trouble brewing down in Rhode Island, and I need your help."

An hour later, the four kids, Bonnie, and her assistant Steven were heading south on Route 146 in Bonnie's minivan. Of course, she refused to acknowledge its minivan ancestry.

"Steven, if you call this a minivan one more time, I'm launching you out the side door," Bonnie yelled out over her shoulder. She turned to Zoe in the front passenger seat. "I have two grown daughters and four fun-loving, rambunctious grandchildren. I love to hike, go camping, and my hobbies often require me to haul a lot of stuff. And I like to go fast. Hence, you are currently riding in my beloved AMG R63 and luxuriously travelling faster than the police would probably care for. All thanks to the power supplied by a recently installed a twin-scroll supercharger on the engine, bringing this puppy just north of 550 horsepower. I even did the wrench work myself."

"Woah," the four kids muttered.

"And, I like the leather seats," Bonnie chimed in.

Mindful of why they were on this trip in the first place, Zoe tried to bring the subject back to the mission. "So, you didn't want to discuss it back in Worcester as you said we were in a rush, but who are you exactly and why are we here?"

"Ah, right, sorry my lass," Bonnie replied. "I was still thinking about getting my butt whooped in that D&D game back there. Conrad can be brutal, huh?"

The kids laughed. They had played plenty of games with Conrad and the rest of the Order this past year since becoming the inaugural members of the Junior Order of Draco. They had a running campaign going and played every Sunday afternoon if they had all their homework done first, of course.

"My name is Bonnie Gold," she continued. "And I am the leader of the Rhode Island chapter of the Order of Draco. We're based in Newport and function similarly to how you and the crew do up in Worcester. Granted, we don't have any fancy-pants sword wielders related to an actual dragon like you guys do, but we manage with what we've got."

This elicited a round of chuckles from the backseat. The kids adored Liam and looked up to him. Whenever it came time for training, research into ancient texts, or even just performing maintenance on the tower, the children hung on his every word and mimicked his actions, hoping to be like him someday.

"This fine gentleman is my second in command, Steven Silver." Turning her head to the side to be better heard, she said, "By the way, we're about fifteen minutes out. Make the call."

"Yes, ma'am." Steven pulled his cell phone out of his pocket and quickly called one of the numbers in his contacts. "Yes," he said, into the device. "The usual. One coffee and the rest chocolate. Yes, six total, please."

Turning back to Zoe, Bonnie continued. "We're based out of the Newport Tower, much like your HQ in Bancroft Tower. Have you seen it before?"

"No, ma'am," Zoe replied. "I've never even been to Rhode Island before today."

"WHAT?!" Bonnie exclaimed. She turned back to the three children in the rear of the vehicle. Her eyes wide, scanning back and forth, she found equal confusion in the sideways shakes of their heads. "You kids have never been down here before? Well, buckle up. You're in for a treat."

Just over fourteen minutes later, Bonnie turned onto Bellevue

Avenue and swung into a parking lot in front of a strip mall. Yanking on the hand lever next to her seat, the carbon-ceramic brakes quickly brought the vehicle to a halt.

"Steven, would you be a dear?" she said, turning and handing the man several green bills. "And bring one of the whelps with you to help carry the cups."

Turning back to Zoe and the two remaining kids, she continued. "Where were we? Oh! Right. The tower. Our base is just a few streets over from here and located in Tuoro Park. Unlike Bancroft Tower in Worcester, which is semi-secluded up on that beautifully wooded hill of yours, ours is right out in the open. So, we needed to be a little creative with our entrance."

The kids looked back at her, clearly puzzled.

"Ooh! I wish that we had time to do a tour right now, but we are on such a time crunch," Bonnie said, trying to assuage their sorrows over not seeing the tower on this trip. "It's built below the remnants of an old Viking lookout post erected shortly after they had landed here. It was originally constructed to keep watch over the ocean for approaching vessels. We've done a good job of staying off the radar of onlookers and almost blew our cover a few years back when some researchers tried to convince everyone that it was actually built by the Vikings! Can you believe that? A few well-placed papers claiming that it was only a mill and a couple quiet payments to make some people go away, and... voila! We have a secret base in the middle of a populated city."

The kids continued to look at her with equal parts confusion and amazement at this lady's nonchalant admission to bribery and forgery.

"Nobody got hurt!" Bonnie exclaimed, sensing their concerns. "Anyway, once you see it, you'll just fall in love with the place."

Just then, the side door slid open, revealing the waiting Steven and Luca. Both were standing there holding drink trays, three drinks each, napkins, and straws.

"Ooh! Give me! Give me!" Bonnie reached out excitedly for her drink. Zoe had seen kids less excited to open presents from Santa on

Christmas morning.

"What is this?" Zoe inquired, taking her cup from Luca.

"This, my friends," Bonnie declared, holding her cup up like a prize on a game show, "Is an Awful Awful. The most delectable concoction of goodness ever created by the hands of man. It is a heavenly mixture of whole milk, flavoring, and frozen ice milk."

"So," Stella began, right before sucking down another long sip from her straw, "Is it just a Cabinet, then?"

"Au contraire, my young apprentice," Bonnie said between chuckles. "You are quite an astute connoisseur of the dairy treats, I can see. But a Cabinet lacks the frozen ice milk, which is what sets this deliciousness apart from the others."

Pulling out of the parking lot once everyone was buckled in and the drinks distributed, Bonnie headed east away from the strip mall down Memorial Boulevard. Looking in her rearview mirror, she squirmed with glee at the sight of the happy faces in the back seat sucking down their chocolatey drinks.

Several minutes later, after pulling off the road and parking at the beginning of a public beach, the crew unloaded from the minivan and piled out onto the sidewalk with cups in hand. Everyone except for Bonnie. Her quickly downed cup sat empty in the console of the AMG.

"My friends!" Bonnie exclaimed over the sound of the crashing waves behind her. "Welcome to Easton Beach. Well, First Beach, as we call it around here."

The kids looked around at the wonders before them. There was a long stretch of sand, restaurants dotting the nearby boardwalk, and a rocky shoreline off to the right that stretched toward the horizon. It was a nice enough beach and all but seemed unremarkable given Bonnie's excitement to come here and the general haste which underlined their actions today. Zoe looked about, her eyes settling on the line of crashing waves at the foot of a collection of mansions off to the right.

"This place is cool," she said to Steven. "Can we go climb on the rocks? I want to look for sea creatures in the water."

"Sure!" Steven replied, looking over to Bonnie and winking. "We will definitely make time for you to go explore and look for some creatures. Hopefully you don't run into anything too scary," he said with an awkward chuckle.

"Ooh!" someone exclaimed behind the group. Zoe looked to see Luca jumping up and down. "I've heard of them before. Dell's! Bonnie, can I go and get a drink?"

Bonnie looked to each of the children to gauge the general thirst of the bunch. They had all just sucked down the thick milkshakes and could probably use something a little more refreshing. She handed him a wad of cash. "Get one for everyone, won't ya?"

"Gee, thanks!" He took off in a flash toward the van strategically positioned at the entrance to the parking lot.

"Now, while we wait for Luca to return, who has heard of the Cliffwalk before?" Bonnie asked, looking from face to face. "No one? Well, you're going to enjoy this then."

Waving them along, she walked the group toward the rocky beach. When they had all arrived (except for Luca who was still in line for lemonade) she turned her back to the water and assumed the role of tour guide.

"This, my young friends, is the Newport Cliffwalk and mansions," she said, picking up the volume to accommodate for the crashing waves. "Starting from the beach here, you can walk 3.5 miles that way and check out some of the oldest and most expensive mansions in Newport. One of them is even still partially occupied by relatives of Anderson Cooper!"

"Who's Anderson Cooper?" Giovanni asked, puzzled.

"What? How do you not know who Anderson Cooper is?" Bonnie exclaimed. "He's that handsome man on the news. His mom is Gloria Vanderbilt herself!"

"Who?" Zoe asked.

Giving up, Bonnie waved them off. Looking up, she waved to Luca who was shuffling down the beach toward the group with two trays in his hands. Reaching out to help him, Bonnie grabbed one of the trays and distributed lemonades to the kids. Taking her own at the end, she took a long sip from the paper cup and let out an exaggerated gasp.

"That really hit the spot," she told the group. Looking from face to face, she could see that they also enjoyed the sugary goodness that was Dell's. "Anyhoo, where was I?"

"Handsome news anchors?" Zoe contributed with a sarcastic shrug.

"Right!" Bonnie said, giving her a wink. "But what I should be getting to is our problem at hand. As you can see, the shoreline is made up of large rocks protecting the higher ground from being eroded away by the relentless pounding of the waves. Without the Cliffwalk being built like this, the ocean would bombard the cliffs and retake what she sees as hers. The city of Newport and the well-to-do owners of these mansions spent considerable time and money years ago to put these boulders in place to protect their investments."

"So, how does that involve us?" Stella asked, looking around and raising her hand. "It seems like everything is okay."

Bonnie nodded in agreement. "You don't waste any time, Miss Stella, do you? Right, let's get to it, then." She led the kids down the beach and onto the beginning of the paved portion of the walk. Leading them along for a few minutes, she kept walking until they had made their way past Seaview Avenue. Looking over the side, they could get a better view of the larger rocks just below the paved walkway. Pausing a moment while she waited for the last of them to catch up, she pointed to the rocks below.

"Approximately forty-eight hours ago we received the first of several tips from police and public authorities who are familiar with the special nature of our charter," Bonnie began. "Some of the officers had witnessed the incidents on their own while others had received notifications from members of the general public. Thankfully, they were on the lookout for this sort of thing and told the callers made up stories about aquatic creatures or some other tomfoolery and to not worry about it."

"Worry about what?" Zoe whispered to Luca. He shrugged back.

"Dragons, my dear," Bonnie said, having overheard Zoe's not-so-quiet whisper. "Two days ago, some dragons— recently hatched whelps, to be exact—were spotted in and around the Cliffwalk right around down there." She pointed down at the rocks just above where the waves were pummeling the shoreline ten feet below.

She watched the four faces look back at her in awe, remarking how excited and nervous they all seemed to be. Except for Zoe. That girl was a spitfire and reminded Bonnie of herself as a young girl.

"From what we can tell, there are some baby dragons hiding amongst the rocks just below our feet," she continued. "We have had plain-clothed scouts patrolling First Beach and the Cliffwalk here trying to see them, but they have yet to have any luck. Water dragon babies, whelps, you know, are typically active at night and have done a good job of evading our detection so far. As you can imagine, it's too dangerous to let them just continue living along the heavily travelled tourist area, so we need to find, capture, and relocate them as soon as possible."

"Relocate?" Luca asked. "What about their mom and dad?"

Bonnie's face warmed as a smiled graced her face. Touching her hands to her heart, she looked down at the young man. "Aw! You are such a dear. With any other creature, this may very well be the case. But this species of dragons lay their eggs in well-hidden locations near sources of food and abandon the eggs once satisfied that the young are prepared to hatch and fend for themselves. It might seem harsh by human standards, but the dragons have lived for millions of years using this methodology, so there must be something to it."

"So, when do we begin?" Zoe asked.

After the sun had set and the beach was cast only in the faint light from the Moon, the group made their way back to the rocks. They had walked up the street to the Cliffside Inn to enjoy the tearoom and raid their pastries and snacks. Steven spent most of the time losing his mind at the appalling notion of mere children committing sacrilege to one of Newport's oldest inns and a landmark in its own right, but Bonnie enjoyed every moment of it. She spent the time chatting with the youngsters trying to learn what made them tick. Over multiple cups of tea and more cucumber sandwiches than she could count, Bonnie learned what each kid enjoyed about the Order, why they stuck with it, and what their special skills were that they felt could aid the organization. She soaked up every detail and filed them away for future use.

While this mission may seem easy compared to other operations conducted by the Order, Bonnie knew that a good plan only lasted until first contact. The second an unknown variable introduced itself and mucked up their plans, she'd need to adapt and pivot to keep things moving and ensure their success. So, if she had to fork over a few hundred dollars to appease the owners of the inn and let her kids dirty up their little tea area, then so be it.

Creeping down the last length of Seaview, Bonnie waved the kids forward and led them to the edge of the Cliffwalk. Looking around to see if anyone was paying attention, she scooted northward on the paved walkway for about fifty feet. Scanning the area one last time, Bonnie gripped the railing with both hands and shimmied herself up and over to the other side.

"Where did she go?" Stella whispered.

"Down there, I guess," Zoe whispered back, loud enough for the rest of them to hear. "Last one down is a rotten egg!"

Mimicking the move of the grownup, Zoe flung herself over the edge into the blackness below. Not to be outdone, she was quickly joined by her three friends.

Ten feet below at the bottom of a grassy slope, the kids brushed the sand from their knees after sliding down to the shoreline. With the water being out due to low tide, the ground was still moist, but they didn't have to stand in the water and get their shoes too wet. Letting their eyes adjust to the low light, they took in the scene and found their leader.

"Wow!" Bonnie exclaimed over the sound of the nearby crashing waves. "You kids aren't afraid of anything, are you?"

The kids smiled, accepting the compliment in silence.

Bonnie's face went from its normal jovial display of dragon-love and adventure-enthusiasm to one of serious contemplation. It was game time.

"Alright," she started, now addressing them as Order operatives. "If you look down here, you can see a gap formed between these two rocks." The woman kneeled into the sand-rock mixture and crawled toward the opening, pointing inward as she moved. "Luca, bring up that flashlight that I gave you and see if you can shed some light on the subject."

The boy laughed at her terrible pun, but secretly loved it. His father was a connoisseur of dad jokes, and he grew to enjoy the dry, often ridiculous style of humor. Crouching before the small cave, Luca pointed the light into the opening and froze as two small orbs reflected light back at him.

In a blur of red and black, a wave of colored scales and wings rushed toward the boy and knocked him back into the water. Three blue dragon whelps, no bigger than a large dog, had leapt from the opening and barreled into the still-stunned Luca. The heads of the creatures frantically darted from face to face of the equally surprised humans gazing down upon them. Three sets of stubby-clawed feet nervously pawed the ground. Then as one, they blasted off in different directions.

"Quick! Catch them!" Zoe yelled out.

She dove toward the closest one to her and came up empty as the wily creature tore through the group and zipped under Bonnie's feet, sending her hurtling to the ground. Reaching down to the woman's outstretched hand, Zoe helped her up and the followed after it, back toward the cave.

One of the two remaining babies zipped directly up the rocky cliffside and jumped onto the walkway above while the other started down the shoreline, heading south. Without saying a word, Bonnie and the three remaining kids broke into two sets of two and chased after the other dragons. Bonnie took Stella with her up the rock wall while Luca and Giovanni ran down the shoreline in pursuit of their quarry.

"Come here, little guy," Zoe whispered into the dark.

She was on her hands and knees crawling through the damp sand, her back scrapping against the top of the tunnel as she progressed. She couldn't tell just how far she had gone, but Zoe knew that she had travelled at least twice her height by now. What concerned her, though, was that she was starting to go downward. Each shuffle forward brought her into wetter areas, and eventually, into standing water.

Pushing Stella up and over the lip of the cliff, Bonnie then pulled herself up and broke into a sprint alongside the young girl. The two raced up Seaview Ave in pursuit of the long blue shadow bounding up the hill, desperate to catch the dragon before it got loose in public.

Yanking the cell phone out of her pocket as they ran, Bonnie flipped through the menus without looking and rang Steven's number.

"Yes! We found them," Bonnie huffed into the microphone. Steven's voice could be indistinctly heard through the speaker. "No, not exactly. They split up. Bring my van around to the top of Seaview and try to block the street... sure, my van, car, whatever, just meet us there!"

They pumped their legs as hard as they could in pursuit of the small creature. Coming up on the parking lot to the Cliffside Inn, Bonnie could just make out the distinct growl of her exhaust racing along Cliff Ave on an intercept course.

"Stella!" Bonnie yelled, pointing to the right as she broke left. "Chase the whelp into the parking lot and scare it back toward me in the street. I have an idea!"

Without question, the young girl careened to the right and ran along the perimeter of the lot. Just as the woman had hoped, the small dragon broke left to avoid the girl and the entrance to the inn. Leaping back out onto the paved street, the dragon was mere feet away from freedom when Bonnie crashed into it, bear-hugging the being as they both shot straight into the open sliding door of her car.

Nearing what had to be the end of the small tunnel, Zoe could hear a new sound over the ever-present crashing of waves on rocks: breathing. Clambering around a rock jutting into the passage from the right, she paused. Up until now, she was able to see from the moonlight reflecting off the water. It was a cloudless night and a full moon, so the team was able to move about so far without drawing extra attention to themselves.

Reaching down to her pockets, she fumbled for a moment, as she tried to slide the flashlight out and before her. She struggled against the device as the edge of the metal light caught inside the hem of her jean pockets. Finally freeing the stubborn thing, she pressed the button and held it before her. There, at the back of the cave, huddled a shivering baby dragon. It had its head buried into the rocks at the end of the passage, but she could see in the dim glow cast by the flashlight that it was occasionally looking back over its shoulder at her.

Taking her time while softly making shushing sounds, Zoe crawled her way toward the scared creature. She had no idea how the little guy would react to her approach, but she needed to get him out now before the tide came in any further. Closing the distance quickly, she brought herself within arm's reach and stopped.

Reaching out with a visibly shaking hand, Zoe extended her arm and hovered her hand just over the small creature's back. Slowly lowering it towards the skin of the adorable little whelp, she gently touched the scales just to the side of its dorsal ridges and stroked back toward herself. The whelp pulled away at first, but then allowed her contact after a very long moment. It looked up at her, and while she wasn't definitively sure, she could have sworn that it smiled.

That is, until the water crashed into them.

Shrieking in surprise as the freezing cold water lapped at the back of her legs, Zoe scared both herself and the whelp as the wave worked its way through the tunnel and splashed into them. It shot past her body and drenched the tiny creature, further throwing it into a fit. She assumed that it could swim but given the multitude of stressors currently ravaging the young being's mind, the wave was probably the last thing that it needed.

The whelp shot back in response, pushing against Zoe's tiny frame, and driving her into the side wall of the tunnel. She tried to wrap her arms around it, but the waves had made everything slippery, and she couldn't find purchase on the dragon's scales. She banged her head into an adjacent rock and dropped the light, plunging her back into darkness. Reeling from the blow, she fought against a sudden feeling of stupor threatening to knock her out.

Feeling the dragon slip past her, she threw her arms out in desperation, both to grab onto the creature and find any rock, stick, anything, anything at all to grab on to and lead her back to the tunnel entrance. Regaining her composure as her brain fought through being rattled against the rock back there, she managed to see through the darkness and found the path once more. Crawling on bruised hands and knees, each advance hurting more than the last, she scurried down the length of the passage, desperately seeking fresh air and the slimy tail of her quarry.

Gaining ground on the impossibly fast whelp, she lurched forward and was just about to grab onto it when she felt a rush of heat race through the muscles of her calf and ankle of her right leg. Struggling to move forward, she looked back in the dim light to see why she couldn't move. A rock had fallen from the side of the tunnel, landing over her leg and pinning her in place. She wasn't going anywhere.

Looking forward, she could see the dragon make it to the end of the tunnel. Its silhouette was eclipsed by the reflected moonlight shining down the length of the tunnel, and for the briefest of moments, she forgot about the pain, impending rush of water, and marveled at how beautiful the creature really was. She didn't know why, and it pained her to ask for it, but she yelled for help. To the dragon.

Turning its head just as it was about to leave, the dragon looked back to her. Perhaps it was only having fun and enjoyed being chased. Maybe it was doing a victory sneer at her failure to catch him. Or maybe, just maybe, it was looking back in sorrow at her predicament. She would never know. The dragon turned back toward the beach and bounded forward.

"Sorry! Oof! My bad!" Luca blurted out a string of apologies for the hundredth time in the last five minutes. At this point, he wasn't even looking at the person to whom he was apologizing. It had simply become a reflexive action while he ran.

And boy, did he run. And dodged broken bits of antique furniture and glass, oddly enough.

After they had chosen their dragon and followed in pursuit, they had quickly discovered that these dragon babies, or at least the one which they had mistakenly picked, couldn't fly yet, but could run like an Olympic marathoner. The little guy had quickly darted down the rocky walkway due south with the two boys in close pursuit. They had passed many houses, more than they could keep track of over the sounds of their hearts beating through their chest, but they knew that they were approaching the more expensive looking homes.

While running, they had hailed Steven on the radio that they were approaching the Salve Regina campus and that they needed help. Giovanni kept in contact with Steven while they ran, which was hard because from the sound of it, the man was busy struggling with something in Bonnie's van, but he somehow managed to keep the boys guided on what to do.

"Try driving the dragon back toward the street," the man calmly stated over the sounds of low growls. "We're coming to you!"

"Boys!" A female voice called out from the speaker, sounding further away. "Get the dragon onto Ochre Point Ave and we'll see you soon!"

"Who was that?" Luca called out over his huffing and puffing.

"I think it was Bonnie," Giovanni replied. "Let's chase it through this yard up ahead and sweep around behind it. We need to get to the road!"

And that was when they realized the tiny yard up ahead was Ochre Court, and that Salve was hosting a rather festive gala that evening. They chased the dragon through throngs of people mingling in the dimly lit lawn, bedecked in their finest and holding fragile glasses and plates. Cries of surprise rang out from amongst the well-to-do attendees as the three party-crashers rushed through the crowd, throwing the scene into absolute chaos.

They pumped their legs as fast as they could go and continued the chase down the path. The dragon began veering back toward the water, so Luca burned ahead on the left while Giovanni dropped back a few feet, hoping to create a tangible wedge to drive the dragon off to the right. The plan finally began to work as the whelp broke off toward a humungous building up ahead.

"Go wide!" Giovanni yelled to Luca. "Let's get him to the road. I can see it just past the mansion."

"Steven, Bonnie, come in," Giovanni called over the radio. "I think that we'll get him out to the street at this house."

"Where are you?"

"I don't know," he replied between breaths. "But this place is huge. It has tan stone walls and a red roof. Do you recognize it?"

"Oh no…" he heard a hushed voice through the radio, followed by the rumble of Bonnie's engine roaring in the background. "You're at The Breakers. Be careful… that place is expensive."

Looking ahead, the boys watched as the blue-black blur of the dragon leapt over a well-kept shrubbery and launched itself through a window in the back wall.

Giovanni looked to Luca for advice and the other simply shrugged. They took off after the whelp, quickly scurrying up the side of the stone wall and through the shattered window. They found themselves in a rather lavish room and continued after the creature, dodging a string of smashed objects in the wake of the scaled intruder. The formerly opulent palace was apparently not designed to handle errant dragons and was now awash in broken glass and shattered artifacts.

Pushing through the mess, the boys rounded a corner as a large painting fell off the wall in front of them, landing on their heads. Carefully hoisting it from themselves by the frame, they looked down at the placard.

"Gloria and Anderson," Luca read. "Hmm. I don't know what Bonnie's talking about. That's not what a silver fox looks like." Giovanni shrugged and leaned the painting up against the wall.

Looking to their right, they saw the dragon burst through another window at the end of the hallway. Running after it, they passed through an adjacent door and outside into the spacious driveway. Heading toward the left where they felt the main road to be, they watched in horror as the dragon bound once, twice, and leapt high over the thick iron gate before them.

Just as their hearts began to sink into their stomachs, they watched in awe as Bonnie's car screeched to a halt on the other side. The sliding door opened with Bonnie and Stella rushing out, tossing a net over the whelp just as it alighted the sidewalk before them. The boys hustled up and over the fence, taking their time now that the chase had thankfully come to an end.

Hands on their knees, they caught their breath as Bonnie lifted the equally exhausted dragon into the back and secured it in the second cage. They could see one cage already holding an angry looking whelp while a third sat empty.

"Great job, boys!" Bonnie said. She looked around, clearly counting the number of kids with her. "Where's Zoe?"

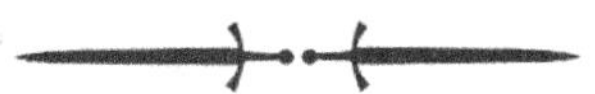

Pulling with all her might, Zoe struggled against the rock pinning her leg in place. While it may have only been a few moments, it felt like she had been stuck for hours. The rising water continued to lap against her and was now almost up to her shoulders. She feared that she would soon find herself with no air to breathe.

But she wouldn't give up.

Despite the pain shooting up the length of her leg, she pulled and yanked against the very earth trying to hold her back. She was breathing harder with the effort and found herself frequently being splashed in the face by a rogue wave. The salty water was freezing and sapped her of her strength, draining what little reserves of energy remained quickly. While she would fight till the end, she had to admit that the end may come sooner than later.

Tugging against the rock, her own leg acting as both her lifeline and ultimate demise, she sucked in a last mouthful of air as the water level rose above her lips. Gritting her teeth, she bent her head forward and searched the flooded tunnel walls for anything to grab on to. Finding purchase on two rugged handholds, she pulled hard against the rock, even as she felt something come down and touch upon the back of her neck.

Hauling against her immobilized leg one last time before she was sure she'd run out of air, she felt herself surge forward through the tunnel, finally breaking free of the unrelenting rock tearing into her skin. The water around her turned red as her own lifeforce pumped into the waters of Easton Bay. Slumping into the water, she couldn't hold herself up any longer. Her muscles had given all that they could, but ultimately had their limits. Feeling her body being pulled from the tunnel toward the cool night air, her mind followed suit and she passed out.

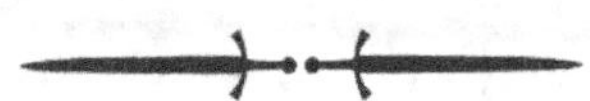

Squinting her eyes against the bright light, Zoe slowly awoke to find herself laying on her back and staring up at the underside of some type of vehicle. She tried to get up but found herself strapped down to a stretcher mounted near the feet of a handful of people. Looking around from face to face, she realized that she was surrounded by her friends. Her face landing on Bonnie's as she heard the woman's voice chime in her ear.

"Good morning, Zoe," she whispered loudly. Zoe could tell that she had tried to speak quietly into her ear via the microphone headsets that they were all wearing but had to speak loudly enough to beat back the sounds from outside. "How are you feeling?"

"Strange," she muttered, looking down at her leg wrapped tightly and held in place. "What happened? Where are we? Why am I strapped down?" Her voice began to rise, panic creeping in as the anxiety of so many unknown variables assaulted her senses.

"Just rest for now, my dear," Bonnie said. "You did well back there, and everything is being taken care of. Sit tight and I'll explain everything to you when we're on the ground."

About an hour later, or so it felt like to the still-groggy Zoe, they touched down at their destination. As the sliding door behind her head opened out of the way, she found herself being lifted up and out of the vehicle by a pair of airmen sporting unfamiliar division badges on their uniforms. Once on the ground, they freed her from the straps and helped her to her feet. One of them proffered a pair of crutches and assisted her in getting comfortable standing upright.

Observing the scene unfolding around her, Zoe watched in amazement as her friends jumped from the sides of the Blackhawk helicopter that they had been flying in. The airmen, along with Bonnie and Steven, were now working on a trio of cages a short distance away. Based on the rigging strewn about the ground, it was clear that they had been tethered to the underside of the chopper and lowered down first upon their arrival.

Quickly figuring out how to properly walk with her new set of crutches, Zoe made her way over to where Bonnie was standing. The woman, having just finished freeing the crates from the camo green cargo webbing, was looking on as the airmen placed each crate on a dolly and started walking them down a path into the woods.

"Zoe!" Bonnie exclaimed, happy to see her. "How's the leg feeling?"

"Good, I think," the girl answered. "What's going on here?" She said, motioning with her hand to the military operators, the helicopter, and the secluded spot in the woods. "What did I miss back there?"

"Well," she started, waving her hand forward, indicating that she'd like to walk in the direction where the others had just disappeared into the greenery. Zoe nodded and they began to walk slowly. "After we caught the first two dragons, we tried to call you on the radio, but couldn't reach you. We raced back to the original spot, guessing that you had chased the whelp into that cavern."

Zoe nodded slowly, taking her time to choose her words. "I tried to get the dragon but failed. I'm sorry, Mrs. Gold," she said quietly. "How did you end up catching it?"

"Catch?!" Bonnie exclaimed, laughing. "We didn't have to catch it at all. When we arrived, we found the whelp pulling you out of the flooded tunnel. He was biting onto the collar of your shirt and dragging you to safety."

"What?!"

Bonnie grinned, shaking her head enthusiastically. "He pulled you right out of the water and onto the dry sand. We couldn't get him to leave your side until the medics arrived and stabilized you. I wouldn't have believed it if I hadn't seen it with my own eyes. He was like a giant puppy laying there next to you, guarding you until he felt that you were safe."

Zoe stared back in amazement. "So, why is he in the cage?"

"Once he realized that you'd be okay and he saw his two clutch mates already secured to be transported, he begrudgingly agreed to join them," Bonnie answered. "It wasn't easy, and there might be a few new scratches on my leather seats, but he ultimately agreed."

"So, what's all this then?"

"This, my dear," Bonnie said, waving her arms around in her best impression of Julie Andrews, "is another one of our secret facilities. My favorite, in fact. We're deep in the heart of northern Vermont, which is all that I'm going to tell you, for now. Few know the place exists and even fewer can reach it. And, thanks to a handful of special inventions which we recently added, is nearly impervious to the spying eyes of planes and satellites from above."

"What do they do here? Are they performing tests on the dragons?" Zoe asked, a frown growing across her face.

"Nope!" Bonnie beamed. "And that's why I love it. This is a sanctuary for green and blue dragons. It's a safe, caring home for all who enjoy water and forest environments with minimal human interaction. We study them, sure, but try to do so without interfering with their lives."

As she spoke, they neared a short cliff overlooking the sanctuary. Zoe could see a large lake being fed by two streams, all of which was surrounded by seemingly endless miles of dark forests with the Green Mountains hovering over them. Looking down at the water, she watched as the three cages were carted to the shoreline.

"Would you like to go down and say goodbye?"

"Goodbye?" Zoe asked, clearly dismayed.

"How about 'bye for now'?" Bonnie inquired. "I'm sure that we can come back up again sometime."

Her smile returning, the two continued down the trail to join the others. At their arrival, Bonnie motioned to the awaiting airmen. As one, they popped the latches on the three cages and jumped back. Everyone watched in earnest anticipation of the dragons tearing from their cages.

Nothing happened.

The humans watched in curiosity as the dragons sat inside, refusing to leave. Zoe crept forward and peeked into the cage closest to her. She immediately recognized her dragon, and to the surprise of her friends, carefully crouched down next to the opening and waited.

Again, nothing happened.

Turning to her friends, Zoe looked up to Luca. "Hey!" she

whispered. "Do you have any snacks?"

Feeling around in his pockets, Luca's face lit up and he extracted a small bag, tossing it to Zoe. She opened the sealed pouch and pulled out a few pieces of beef jerky. Holding her hand out in front of the cage, she waited.

Before she could begin to question the efficacy of her plan, a small blue nose poked out from the opening, sniffing the air. She instinctively flinched, causing the nose to disappear back into the cage. Composing herself, she confidently stuck her out once more. A moment later, she felt a tiny wet tongue swipe the treat from her palm.

Slowly retracting her hand, which was now coated in a thin layer of drool, she put another piece of the meat into her palm and stuck it out again, this time in front of the cage but out in the light. The nose came out once more, this time followed by a complete head and shoulders of the baby dragon. It delicately removed the jerky again, this time looking up to Zoe with the hint of a smile on its face.

Holding out the rest of the bag, Zoe giggled as the whelp plunged its head in and deftly removed any last trace of Luca's food. Looking back up at her, it quickly darted toward her face and licked her cheek. Pulling back, it stared up at her once more before turning and diving into the calm waters of the lake.

Seeing their brother swimming under the surface and popping its head back up a dozen feet out, the two remaining whelps leapt from their cages and followed in his wake. Clambering back to her feet, Zoe supported herself on the crutches as she watched three sets of heads, wings, and swishing tails bolt toward the center of the lake, disappearing below the surface from view.

DRAGON LANCE

"Dragon Eye reporting in. Over," the voice crackled from the headphones worn by the two officers watching the wall of video feeds.

The audio clarity would usually be better given the advanced nature of their equipment, but the speaker was several hundred kilometers away and the pair was listening from their secluded lab in the heart of a mountain. All things considered, the Colonel was impressed with the setup.

"Roger, Dragon Eye," the senior officer replied. "Standby for start of test. Subject within range in five minutes."

The man reached a hand to his ear and pressed the mute button on the side. He rotated the microphone boom to its vertical orientation, as well, to add some insurance that he wouldn't be overheard. Despite using microphones such as these for years, he still didn't trust that the button would actually mute his microphone feed and not transmit his words for the world to hear. A paranoid individual by nature, it was his distrust in everything, and most people, which had kept him alive for so long.

"So, my dear, what do you have for us this morning?"

Dr. Stacy Anastasio, code name Sun Sister, turned to look at the man and dramatically rolled her eyes. She had spent the better part of a year organizing this side project for the Colonel, devoting more than her usual level of attention due to the promising nature of this technology. As the director of this particular R&D wing within the Program's wide array of experimental splinter cells scattered across the globe, Stacy had to ensure the success of every one of her projects, but typically gravitated toward one or two pet projects at a time. This one was her current baby.

"Do you even read my damn memos anymore?" she said, with a snarky edge to her voice not usually permitted by other members of the organization.

He shot her a look.

Taking a deep breath, she straightened. "Sir."

He relaxed and burst into laughter. "Of course, I do! Of course. Dr. Anastasio—Stacy—you always provide me with the most scrumptious of gadgets and new tech for our operatives. I have just been dealing with some concerns over at one of our Vermont bases and am running low on mental energy."

She quickly sobered up, realizing what he was alluding to. "Middlebury?"

The Middlebury facility had been one of the first projects where she had taken the managerial reigns. It had been a rather far-fetched endeavor and she looked back on the work rather fondly. Given their high level of secrecy, the work carried out, and the fact that they performed it all underneath a bustling town without any loose ends fraying, spoke volumes to her leadership skills and the dedication of the personnel under her command. It had been a logistical nightmare and she still found it surprising that they had completed it as designed.

The Colonel could see the concern on her face and understood her dilemma. "It's better that you don't know. But fear not; all is under control, and it does not reflect negatively on you or anything you oversaw those years back."

She frowned. Stacy wasn't used to being kept in the dark, but she also understood the importance of consolidating resources and minimizing information leakage. It was just hard, because, as far as she knew, she was Richard's closest confidant.

"It's just something going on with a new species variant, that's all," he said, trying to assuage her fears and put her mind at ease. "But that's neither here nor there. Let's get back to today's test, shall we?"

Visibly gulping, she nodded and accepted his request. The

rational part of her brain told her that there was no point in worrying over something which she could not control nor had anything tangible to do with, but the emotional part of her brain, or heart, severely disagreed with her pragmatic assessment.

Taking a deep breath, she proceeded, "Today we are proceeding with test number three of the Dragon Lance project. Dragon Lance, as you'll obviously recall from your intensive review of the project's executive summary that I forwarded to you earlier, is an emulation of Project Thor tested by the military during the Cold War."

Ignoring the jab thrown in there about reviewing the executive summary, which he briefly skimmed while on the flight from Vermont to North Dakota, he nodded in understanding. While he was just a boy at the time, he had learned quite a bit about the kinetic bombardment program developed to capitalize on the growing number of satellites orbiting the Earth and our ability to strap all sorts of weaponry to their platforms.

"The program where the military would theoretically," he said while making air quotes signs with his fingers, "deploy telephone pole sized cylinders of tungsten from orbital platforms to drop onto unsuspecting targets down here on the surface?"

"Correct," Stacy replied. "Due to the high-altitude, gravity-assisted acceleration of the mass, the rods, which were originally proposed to be around twenty feet long and one foot in diameter, would reach impact velocities of almost Mach 24."

The Colonel let out a long whistle.

"Then, based on the altitude of the target, local weather patterns, and the resultant air friction along the smooth shaft of the mass, it could impact at speeds between Mach 8.8 – 10.0. It could be devasting to any ground target within minutes of launch and be nearly impossible to detect or thwart until it was too late."

"God, I miss the Cold War," the Colonel muttered. "There was so little red tape to get in the way of making the really cool stuff, you know? Not everything needs to go through oversight committees and budget reports. It nearly takes all the fun out of militaristic global domination."

Stacy shook her head, rolling her eyes.

"Oh hush," he said. "You know you love this stuff just as much as I do."

"I love having a nearly unlimited budget where I can expand the possibilities of scientific advancement and our understanding of the Universe around us. What you do with it afterwards is up to you."

"Anyhoo, let's get back on topic," the Colonel said, trying to change the subject.

He'd never admit it, but she was the closest person in his life and if he were to ever actually tell someone that he loved them, it would be her. Another time, another place, perhaps.

"So, how does Project Thor play into your latest creation?"

"When Project Thor was being developed," she proceeded, "they were mainly concerned with simply slamming as much matter into the ground as fast as physically possible. Their scientists developed the right geometry, selected the proper material to handle the burn during reinsertion, and let the planet's gravity do the rest.

"While some military brass wanted to insert conventional explosives in the midsection of the mass to do the targeted damage, the thinkers in the group were able to convince the less scientifically literate of the bunch that a hurtling mass of solid tungsten going Mach 10 was more than ample to make any of their desired targets disappear from the face of the Earth. This dramatically simplified the design and made the overall functionality of the system more robust. From my contacts on the other side of the fence, I've heard that the simple move from explosives to solid metal increased their success rates by over 50% during live-fire testing."

"But we're not doing that, are we?" The Colonel inquired. The excited curiosity emanating from his words left little to the imagination of just how much he was anticipating her next words.

"Oh, come now, Richard. You know me better than that," she said with a little wink. "Do you really think that I would fly you all the way out here just to show you a hunk of metal slam into the ground."

He smiled, one of his rare ones lately. "And that's why I keep you around. So, what do you got? Hit me with the good stuff!"

"I thought that you'd never ask," she said as she hit a key on her laptop.

A projector mounted to the wall hummed to life, blasting the darkened wall with colored light. As the image came into focus and the man's eyes adjusted to the change in illumination, he saw a presentation slide bearing the following:

Project Dragon Lance – Critical Design Review Presentation
Eyes Only

Timing his reading, Dr. Anastasio clicked a button on the keyboard and advanced to the next slide. She continued to do so for the remainder of the presentation, watching with contained elation as his eyes darted from one factoid or classified photograph to another. She hated to admit it, but this was literally what she lived for: designing cool, innovative technologies that brought joy and amusement to Colonel Richard Garfield.

Half-way through, he held up a finger. "But how does it—"

"Keep reading," she said, advancing to the next slide.

"But—"

Click.

"Ah, okay," he muttered. "But you can't possibly expect—"

Click.

"So, it really stays asleep the whole ti—"

Click.

"Okay, that could theoretically work. But doesn't this violate the terms of agreement outlined in the SALT II or START I arms treaties?"

She laughed. "When has a piece of paper signed by some weak-spined politicians ever stopped you before?"

He smirked, looking over at her out of the corner of his eye. He really did love her. It's unfortunate that he could never tell her. The Colonel had learned years ago that to properly perform a job such as his, you had to be married to the job, not just work it. Heavy was the crown and such.

"Well, alright then," he said, taking a deep breath. "Let's do this."

"Affirmative," she said, looking down at her watch. She clicked the microphone on. "Dragon Eye, this is Sun Sister. Launch commencing in T-minus ten, nine, eight...

1,950 km above the rolling waves of the mid-Pacific, a small red light blinked to life on an otherwise dead looking satellite. Located high above the conventional orbital levels of most other artificial satellites in LEO, this one was positioned with the intent of not being discovered by nosey members of the space community. With multiple space-faring countries developing anti-satellite technologies, whether publicly or secretly, it was important to remain vigilant to intrusion or destruction.

Appearing to be an elongated asteroid, the outer surface was comprised of a radar absorbing skin similar to that used on stealth fighter craft. The surface geometry was developed to minimize its profile from Earth-based observatories, and with a maximum diameter along its length of only ten meters, it was difficult to observe even through conventional telescopes. Additionally, large portions of the side of the body were covered in Vantablack in the hopes of fooling any sensors, cameras, or curious astronauts looking with the naked eye. The material, comprised of billions of miniscule carbon nanotubes, was capable of absorbing nearly one hundred percent of light in the ultraviolet, visible, and infrared spectrums.

Which is why, for the past year and the time spent to launch and position the satellite, this particular celestial body remained undetected and left on its own high above our heads. The team on the ground couldn't even use passive scanning without fear of detection, so they sat in anxiety-ridden communication silence. They didn't know if the satellite had been damaged, detected, or compromised in any way since its final packaging test before it left their lab for the launch pad. Whether this worked or not all boiled down to how dedicated the quality team had been with their validation procedures and the health of the creatures on board.

After receiving the initial power-up signal from the ground control operators, the satellite's batteries began to pump current through the onboard heaters, slowly bringing the ice-cold vessel back to life. When the space within had reached its programmed minimum threshold, an actuator in the rear pushed outward on a hinged section of the outer hull. One-fourth of the outer surface crept outward and revealed a silver tube hidden beneath the thin membrane. Like a flower petal opening to the morning sunlight to begin feeding for the day, the hatch sprung outward. Once clear, the silver tube slid outwards away from the central axis of the craft until the long fins protruding from the polished surface had cleared the protective stealth housing.

And there it hung. A long, thin tube of silvery tungsten shining in the black of space, awaiting its voyage back to Earth.

"Are you ready?" Dr. Anastasio asked the Colonel.

"Let's do this," he said, the grin growing in width across the cleanly shorn skin of his face that only came with years of strict military routine and structure.

Checking the display before her, Stacy confirmed that all sensors were registering properly and that she had received a positive ready-status from the major crew leads. Staring down at a sea of green lights before her, she checked everything once again, finally straightening to her full height when she was satisfied.

"Ground control, this is Sun Sister. We are go for launch. Dragon Lance Test 001 commencing in ten, nine, eight, seven, six, five, four, three, two, one. Launch!"

Her thumb, hovering just over the smooth plastic surface, drove down into the push button, sending an electrical signal through the thousands of miles of wiring running through the lab until it found home in the communications relay to the satellite.

Looking up to the monitors above their station, Stacy and

Richard watched in awe as their latest creation flared to life. Standing shoulder to shoulder, Stacy's hand moved out ever so slightly in search of Richard's. Sensing the hairs on the side of his fingers, a wave of exhilaration shot through her veins. She had yearned for this moment for so long, craved his touch, or even just the smallest hint of humanity beyond the hyper professional soldier that he convinced everyone that he was.

But there was more to him, she knew it. She was about to reach out, about to extend not only her hand but the daring of her personal and professional livelihood. Once she made contact, they could never go back to the way things were before. Her pinky crept out, angling from her hand toward his, but stopped. She pulled her hand back to her side, almost hard enough to make a slapping sound. Had he heard? Did he feel her presence? She did not know and never could.

It was never meant to be.

With the click of the tube's clamps being released and an eerily quiet puff of compressed nitrogen, the tube crept forward toward the blue sphere before it. Carefully metered and filled months ago on earth, the nitrogen shot out of the cold gas thruster, launching the vehicle forward and rapidly accelerating it into the clutches of Earth's gravitational pull. Slipping through the near vacuum of LEO, the cylinder raced downward, heading toward the target far below.

Entering the upper reaches of the atmosphere, the tube was travelling in excess of 6,805 m/s as it finally began to feel the effects of atmospheric drag against the highly polished tungsten surface. The material, chosen for its extremely high melting point, pushed its way through the atmosphere, compressing the air before it until it superheated to almost 3,000°F. What should have melted nearly any other material trying to reenter in this fashion only slowed the tube down. Plunging through the thin air, the tube's target slowly came into view by the internally mounted onboard sensors.

Racing toward the dusty terrain below, the tube flashed downward through the early morning sunlight like a flash of lightning. Flames raced along the side of the vessel, streaking behind it like the tail of a comet. The outer surface wasn't melting, but gases, particulate, and everything else encountered by the object as it plunged toward the Earth flared to nothingness in its wake.

It did, however, absorb some of the heat. Nestled inside the confines of the silver tube, just below the relatively thin shell of the structure, slept a being of tremendous power. Deep chilled to the point of hibernation back in the laboratory, the creature was slid into the hollow chamber and secured to the rear section of the structure. Kept in a state of deep slumber until launch, the heat from atmospheric insertion slowly woke the being as it descended from the heavens. Nearing consciousness several miles above the surface, the creature finally opened its groggy eyes.

And screamed.

Microphones and cameras within nose end of the tube, positioned behind hardened thermal barriers to protect their delicate sensors from dragonfire and gnashing teeth, recorded the moment in which the being realized where it was trapped. Having lost consciousness back in its cell within one of the Program's secret facilities, it was just now realizing that while it was unsure of its current location, it did know that it was trapped, utterly confused, and hotter than even its heat resistant scales were accustomed to.

It wanted out, and it wanted out immediately.

"Holy sh—"

"Sir?!" Stacy muttered, giving the Colonel some serious side eye.

"I'm sorry, but you're watching the same thing I am, right?" he said, the bewildered amazement dripping from his voice. "You packed a pissed off dragon with what I can only imagine to be a severe case of a head rush inside of a three-foot diameter metal tube and now it wants to get out. This is amazing!"

Turning away, she allowed herself a smile. The man was very hard to please and was known for always finding something wrong with even the most successful of projects. To get this reaction, albeit completely out of character and unbecoming of an officer of his stature, tickled the woman pink. Composing herself, she turned back to the Colonel and the status screens before them.

"If you are enjoying that, then watch this," she said, pressing the button on the side of her helmet. "Dragon Eye, do you have a visual on the subject?"

"Confirmed, ma'am," the voice crackled through the speakers in their ears. "Subject is at 40,000 feet and falling. Vehicle is slowing down at an acceptable rate tolerance and appears to be on track for an impact within the acceptable limits of the target."

"Roger," she replied. "Continue recording and report any anomalies."

"Roger."

Reaching down to the control panel before her, Stacy flipped up a cover guarding an illuminated toggle switch. She stepped back and motioned to the panel, extending a hand toward the awaiting controls.

"Would you like to start the show?"

Grinning like a little kid at a toy store, he stepped forward, smiling down at the woman. "It would be my honor," he said, reaching forward and thumbing the switch forward.

An instant later, a sky-blue jumble of cloth and cord shot out from the rear end of the tungsten tube, quickly unfurling into a small parachute. Smaller than a standard chute used to safely lower a pilot to the ground after an ejection, this chute was deployed simply to slow the fall of the subject attached to it. The subject in question wouldn't be landing on the ground and could benefit from a little extra boost in speed during its descent.

The Colonel continued to watch the live feeds from both the inside of the tube and the camera held by Dragon Eye as the scene unfolded at the test site. The front portion of the tungsten vehicle, freed from the restrictive rear half connected to the parachute, plummeted downward toward the building below. The target, a mock office building constructed by a special contractor for use in this clandestine operation, held no personnel, utilities, nor anything else required to function. What it did hold, however, was the hardened structural components used in modern buildings and a sophisticated array of sensors and cameras monitoring the proceedings. The visuals and data coming out of the building in the following few minutes would decide whether the funding for this project would continue to flow from the Colonel's sources. They were awfully skittish when it came to untested technologies and preferred to work with tried-and-true weapons of old.

But old tech was boring, the Colonel continued to remind them, and made sure to not fail when it came to delivering results. That's why he had made it as far as he had in life and for so long. And when it did not work? Well, he just made sure that he wasn't standing there without a chair when the music stopped.

Looking at the feed coming from Dragon Eye's camera, Richard and Stacy watched in awe as the forward section of the tube slammed into the roof of the building. Between the mass of the tungsten rod and the speed that it was travelling at impact, the upper portion of the building crumbled and shot outward, decimating anything and everything that would have been on the upper three floors. The mass continued to burrow down into the lower levels of the construction until it slammed into the second subbasement thirty feet below grade.

"Woo!" the Colonel yelped.

Stacy smiled at the man, pleased as always when one of her experiments produced this sort of reaction from the man. Looking down at her live readouts coming through the monitors, she pushed the glasses back up her nose and put her game face on.

"Projectile penetration at thirty-four feet below ground level elevation, which is thirty-three percent less than we achieved with a solid mass body during initial testing," she said, continuing to read and mentally calculate the comparisons. "Kinetic energy transfer from mass to building materials appears to have dropped by almost forty percent. Seems acceptable given the change in rod design and our intended result for the final weapon."

"Hmm, not bad," the Colonel muttered. He was listening to her report and legitimately interested in her conclusions, but he had a hard time focusing while watching the camera's feed trained on the rear section. "Come on, break free. You can do it!"

As if the dragon could hear him, the creature flung its silvery arms out wide, bursting forth from the curved metal panels enveloping the length of the creature. Designed to hold the being in place during loading and to prevent it from getting injured when the two halves separated, the titanium-reinforced carbon fiber structures shattered under the forceful thrust of the creature's muscles. Flinging them wide, the falling assembly began to wobble as the geometrical characteristics of the outer shell changed rapidly. The wind resistance pulled on the panels, ripping whatever was left of them off and out into the blue beyond. Looking upward, they could see the creature gazing into the underside of the cone at the tip, put in place to help the vehicle slip through the lower atmosphere after losing its dense forward section. Pushing off from its bindings on its legs and shoving the thin cone around and off its head, the dragon was finally freed from its plummeting prison.

Frantically wobbling in midair as it fell in excess of 100 mph, the creature found its bearings and tucked into a sharp dive, its shimmering wings wrapped around its body as it shot through the air like a living missile. The dragon was of the primal variety, a non-sapient being which lived and died according to its animalist urges and needs. Unlike the other dragons created through the introduction of a soul into the egg during dormancy, this dragon wanted nothing more than to survive at any cost.

Of course, Sun Sister's lab had helped with that, a little. When the dragon was younger, it had been carefully conditioned to follow a basic set of commands. Through a variety of highly classified stimuli, the dragon could be told to fly, eat, sleep, and other basic life functions which the creature already knew how to do. Additionally, and this was found out almost by accident, the creature could be commanded to attack a specified target if it were shown a photo of the person or location while suffering a mild amount of pain. They had tested this on several occasions under strictly controlled environments at one of their facilities, but never through the Dragon Lance.

Until now.

Prior to being inserted into the vehicle, several images of the building were projected onto the walls of the creature's cell while it had received some minor shocks mixed with a few weeks' worth of starvation. Some might say it was cruel to make the dragon suffer like this, but the results were extraordinary and hard to duplicate via other means. Stacy had once hated these types of experiments, but that girlish naivete left in her tired heart had died long ago in the pursuit of success.

The two officers watched in awe as the dragon unfurled its wings several hundred feet from the rooftop of the building and swooped out of the way in a wide arc. The rear section of the tungsten tube, still falling behind it at a slower rate of decent from the parachute, suddenly shot forward as the chute's strings were cut. It picked up speed and slammed into the poured concrete upper level of the structure, puncturing through, and smashing into what was left of the higher portions of the building. The dragon, swinging around in a wide arc, turned back to face the edifice and began its attack run.

Pumping its shining, leathery wings, it poured on the speed and came in close to the bottom floor of the building. As it approached, it opened its mouth, exposing two long rows of sharply pointed teeth eclipsing a raging fire burning at the back of its throat. With a puff of its lungs, the beast blasted the outer walls of the edifice, scorching all flammable materials in the process. As it passed windows and doorways, the fire burst through their openings and pummeled the interior walls, floors, and ceilings, further lighting the building aflame.

Swooping past the edge of the structure, the dragon arced upward, and turned around for another pass. Through the camera feed coming from Dragon Eye, the two in the lab watched in silence as the dragon continued to blast the exterior of the building, laying waste to anything and everything in its path. At one point, the dragon seemed interested in something inside of an open window. They watched in utter curiosity as the thing perched itself along the window frame, digging its claws deep into the brick exterior to hold on. Sticking its head inside, they could see it sniff around for a moment before arching its neck back. It looked around for a moment, as if it were expecting something, or someone, to be coming for it while it lay vulnerable during its attack. Clearly not sensing any imminent threat, the dragon leaned back into the opening and belched a massive plume of fire into the room beyond. The resultant blast from the superheated air within was so great that a massive pressure wave burst forth from the windows on the other side of the building, spraying the ground below with shards of glass and window trim.

Pushing off from the side of the crumbling concrete, the dragon took to the air and hovered around the perimeter of the building. The keen eyes of the apex predator scanned the grounds below, looking for any movement from additional targets. Not seeing anything, the creature immediately calmed down and began to drift away, signaling that it was done with its attack.

"Uh ah ah," the Colonel tsked from back in the control room. "We're not done yet, little one."

The man reached down to the controls and clicked through a series of commands. Pulling up the neural displays and controls on another monitor, he jabbed at a button several times, grinning with glee.

"That'll wake him up," he said, turning to Stacy.

She rolled her eyes, clearly annoyed at the man's flagrant disregard for the health of the creature at the other end of the sophisticated network. While she wouldn't break a sweat maiming or killing a dragon for a crucial test, she didn't do so lightly or on a whim. She valued each and every one of the creatures under her command. One might see this as touching, but the icy blood flowing through her veins did little to warm her heart. She valued them, but only as the ultra-rare and grossly expensive assets that they were to the Program.

Watching through their display screens, they could see the head of the dragon begin to twitch, it's neck craning to its back left as it struggled to deal with the effects of the remote stimulus. Their scientists had long ago determined the optimal nerve clusters to trigger deep within a dragon's brain to warrant a desired action. The Colonel had sent a few volts of persuasion into one such area within this dragon's brain, causing its blood pressure to spike as its emotions boiled from within its core. The enraged beast looked for something, anything to destroy, and dove back into the billowing smoke cloud rupturing toward the sky from the pile of ruins below the dragon's clawed feet.

The creature swooped down and around, clearing the blinding smoke and lining up for another attack run on the structure. The few windows and doorways left from the previous assaults were quickly scorched and hurtled back inside the building. Huge gouts of brilliant orange flames licked out from every opening, venting dark, acrid dust clouds and flaming bits of debris into the hot air beyond.

Feeling the unrelenting pulses from the communications device welded to several scales on its back, the dragon roared in anguished annoyance from the meddling humans. It was nestled just between its two wings where the creature could not reach, leaving it beholden to the whims of the electrical signals from the little device. And so, the dragon continued to pummel the building with fire attacks, flaming salvos of super-heated air, and even a few well-placed slashes from the razor-sharp claws on its hands.

With a lack of flammable materials left for it to destroy combined with the continued onslaught of stimuli wracking its brain from the control unit, something finally snapped deep within the mind of the primal dragon. It began to erratically fly around the space above the wreckage randomly shoot flames of uncontrolled fury this way and that, clawing at invisible demons swooping around it through the smoke-laden air. Back in the control room, the Colonel laughed with glee at the result of his torment.

"Sun Sister," the voice of Dragon Eye crackled through the speaker. "The subject is acting irrationally and could prove to be a danger to both me and our equipment. Over."

Stacy looked up at Richard. "Are you done torturing that dragon?" she asked, glaring into his eyes. No one else in the entirety of their organization could get away with a question like that, and she knew it. She also knew that her leeway with the man had its limits, and it would be dangerous for her to find out where her freedom ended. "I think that it's had enough."

Looking down at her, the smirk on the man's face diminished as he straightened. Play time was over. He lifted his finger from the control panel and ceased firing signals into the creature's mind. Watching in awe for one final moment, he marveled at how the shining surface of the creature's scales reflected the light from the sun in a thousand different directions. It was almost as if its head were one gigantic disco ball... if disco balls could breathe fire and eat people.

"My apologies, Sun Sister," he said, using her code name and not the familial first names that they often used with one another. The change was subtle, but she caught it. "I believe that I have seen enough. Have you collected sufficient data from this test for your current needs?"

"I have, thank you."

"Very well," he said, turning his microphone back on. "Dragon Eye, please standby. Test to conclude momentarily. Continue collecting visual observations and transmit all collected data to our server here at the lab. Acknowledge upon completion."

"Roger, sir."

The Colonel placed his hands upon the keyboard and quickly tapped out a series of commands. Pulling up a new menu, one which Sun Sister had never even seen, he punched several numbers into the keypad before placing his thumb over a fingerprint scanner on the side of the computer.

"Test ending in three, two, one, go," he said out loud, but mostly to himself.

With the push of a button, the next phase of the Colonel's experiment went into action. Stacy had originally protested this aspect of the test, but she ultimately relented when presented with the logical benefits of this technology's application and how it could further their goals. Once again, she sold out her personal morals to advance her career.

Prior to loading the dragon into the tungsten tube, the dragon's scales were coated with a thin layer of liquid magnesium and quickly sealed with a hydrophobic coating. The coating would prevent water and humidity in the air from interacting with the magnesium layer for as long as it remained in place. However, thanks to their crack team of chemical engineers on the payroll, the coating was degraded under an applied current. As the Colonel pushed the button on his controls, a massive capacitor sitting on the dragon's back flared to life and discharged its potential across the skin of the dragon.

Now, one may think that the dragon would be electrocuted at this point, but this sub-species of dragons actually had an innate immunity to anything under a direct lightning strike. The coating, however, did not.

As the electricity arced across the dragon's scales, the protective coating quickly dissipated, leaving the raw magnesium exposed to the atmosphere. Naked and exposed to the elements, the dragon flailed about in the air, writhing in agony as the residual pain from the Colonel's previous torture combined with the annoyance of the normally non-lethal electrical currents wrapping their way around its scaley form. Churning the thick, humid air as it struggled to cope with the ongoing onslaught of electrical and physical pains attacking the poor creature's form, the magnesium layer on the scales finally found a dense pocket of oxygen-rich air rising from the dark forest growth below.

And that is when the dragon lit up like a supernova.

Water, oxygen, and magnesium finally met and did what they did best. Burn hot and blow up. Covering its entire body, the dragon's skin flared to life, thrusting white hot light out in every direction, momentarily blinding those who came to watch the ultimate demise of these newcomers to their woods. The magnesium, mixing with the oxygen and water vapor in the air, burned white hot, enveloping the unsuspecting creature in its own personal, momentary Hell.

Shielding their eyes from the worst of the fiery conflagration, Richard and Stacy turned back to the monitor just in time to watch the remains of the dragon drift down to the ground below, nothing more than a cloud of ash and smoke. Letting out a little laugh and trying not to look at the disgusted look on Stacy's face, the Colonel tapped the microphone once more.

"Dragon Eyes, were you able to capture that on video?"

"As much as I could, sir," the man in the field replied. "The light emission overwhelmed the digital processor on the camera for a moment, despite being almost a klick away, but it momentarily closed the iris in time to prevent any damage. The camera is once again actively filming and uploading in real time for your review."

"And the data?" Stacy asked, excitedly.

"All sensors are active, ma'am," Dragon Eyes replied after a pause, checking the readouts on his laptop. "You should be seeing everything that I'm seeing."

Looking to Stacy and receiving the nod which he was hoping for, the Colonel resumed talking with the operative.

"Great work, soldier," the Colonel began. "Wipe the drive on your computer and activate the transponder on your personal radio. Acknowledge when ready."

"Roger. Please standby."

As the man waited, the Colonel reached down to his keyboard and typed in a series of commands. Entering his personal code once more when prompted by a level five program, he moved his hand down to another covered toggle switch. Gently lifting the cover guard upward, he gingerly traced his thumb along the edge of the switch, preparing himself to activate it.

"Data is wiped from all devices and transponder is active," Dragon Eye stated through their headphones. "Ready to move on your command, over."

Flipping the switch with his thumb, the Colonel watched from afar as the transponder, which in this case was playing double duty as a communications relay to the detonator in the man's pack, triggered the pound of C4 hidden inside the housing of the device. The explosion tore through the man's body, spraying blood and gore upwards of ten meters in all directions. The camera, sitting in front of the operative, was thrown to the side, smashing into a nearby pile of rocks. The equipment was obliterated beyond recognition, destroying what little evidence remained of their experiment. The feed instantly cut out on the other end, presenting Richard and Stacy with a screen full of black and white static.

Reaching into his pocket, the Colonel extracted an alcohol wipe and proceeded to quickly wipe down the buttons, switches, and screens which he had touched during the experiment and observations. Neatly folding the wipe back into the foil packaging and slipping them into his pocket, the Colonel turned to face his scientific counterpart.

"Well, my dear," he started, "another successful test helmed by the legendary Sun Sister. Thank you."

"The pleasure was all mine," she said beaming.

He turned and began to walk down the length of the room toward the only door to the area. Placing his hand upon the doorknob, he turned back to her over his shoulder.

"How much does each launch cost us?"

"Sir, it depends on level of secrecy, how much you want to clean up afterward, specific dragon species—"

"Well, whatever it is," he said, nonchalantly. "Please go ahead and create two additional satellites, fully stocked. Spare no expense."

OH, BOTHER

Tucking his wings close to his body, Tryggvi felt himself begin to drop and nosed downward. Leaning into the fall, he allowed himself to tilt to the right, gently rotating through a quick spin. Barreling forward with his momentum, he descended several wingspans in altitude, just enough to clear the bank of clouds before him. Scanning the ground below and spotting his desire, he unfurled his wings once more, relishing the feel of the strong winds pulling at his taut muscles and arresting his speed. He leaned to the right, bringing himself through a long, slopping arc toward the dark green patch on the horizon.

Racing along the wispy undersides of the lazily drifting stratocumulus clouds, Tryggvi watched as the rocky slopes below began to give way for the dark greens, purples, and shadowy blacks of his hunting ground for the day. From what he could remember going back to the days of his long-lost humanity, the region was known as The Hundred Acre Wood. Not that he could remember why, as the area was rather large and much grander in scale than a simple streamside village, but it was a quaint spot of Earth, nonetheless. Swooping through a long banking turnover and around a tall hill, he brought himself in closer to what he had flown out here.

It was a small patch of trees nestled between a row of hills that featured several species of hardwoods surrounding a small pond and an adjacent grassy clearing. It was this latter area that most intrigued the dragon this fine day. Tryggvi had come out here many times over the past centuries but had abstained in recent history. Whereas the region used to be abundantly populated with a whole smorgasbord of tasty woodland creatures, it had been heavily saturated with a mouse infestation. The mice had held onto the domain for the better part of ninety-five years, driving others away from their carefully guarded property.

Now, however, with the control of the mice dwindling, other creatures were allowed to come in and flourish. Depending on the weather and the activities of the wee creatures who called this place home, the clearing was either a great place to take a nap in the bright afternoon sun, an easy spot to pick up some snacks, or if he was lucky... a little of both.

Circling the clearing from high above, he squinted his scale-lined eyes and zoomed in on the land below. He waited patiently as his eyes adjusted to the newly demanded focal point change, changing the tiny, blurry images below into high-definition previews of his lunch. From what he could see, there was a young pig, an odd-looking yellow bear, and some smaller quadruped rummaging around in the nearby bush. Tryggvi licked his lips, running the long, red muscle over the points of his teeth as he dreamed of the flavors to come. During his last visit, he had gorged himself on a family of rabbits, a gigantic owl, and something called a heffalump. In the years since, he would occasionally have dreams of that particular day and could still imagine the exquisite taste and tantalizing aroma of the scorched flesh from that odd looking elephant-like creature. The muscular meat from its trunk, when roasted just right in a steady stream of promethium, melted in your mouth like butter.

Once, many years ago, he had even managed to nab a seemingly out-of-place tiger. He didn't know how such a creature came to be in the woods in that part of the country, but he didn't let that stop him from enjoying the savory orange and black striped flesh. When you've been alive for as long as Tryggvi had, it was common to go years, even decades, between new and interesting dining options to satisfy one's cravings. He had yet to see another one of these striped creatures but was always careful to keep an eye out for another one should it cross the path of his hungry teeth.

Continuing to circle the patch of green far below, he angled downward, dropping in height a little more with each passing orbit.

As he broke through the last layers of the low-lying clouds, he was finally able to listen in on the sounds of the forest below. There, just a wingspan outside of the tree line along the edge of the small clearing, he found his next meal. Riding the warm air coming up off the warm forest below, he angled himself downward and listened as he approached. It was difficult at first, but the cacophony of sounds began to separate into distinct words and phrases as he made his approach. Straining to listen over the roar of the winds whipping past his ears, he made out the following...

"Oh, bother. Looks like I won't be having any honey today."

"Why's that, Pooh?"

"Well, Piglet, normally I would ask Owl to grab the beehives for me higher up in the tree where they keep their honey—"

"Oh... right. I miss Owl."

"I miss Owl, too, little Piglet."

"Maybe I can help!"

"That would be nice, my little friend. But I am afraid that I am too big for your tiny body. I would probably squish you."

"Ah, you're right, Pooh. Wait! Who's that coming through the thicket? I think that it's a deer."

"Oh, dear."

"No, Pooh, a deer."

"Oh, bother. I've never been good with homonyms, little Piglet."

"Hi there! My name's Bambi. I'm looking for my mother. Have you seen her?"

"Hi, Bambi. I am sorry, but we have not seen another deer. Would you like some honey with me? If we can get it, that is."

"Sure! What can I do to help?"

"Well, it's awfully high up in that tree, and we are too short to reach it without our friend, Owl. Can you reach it?"

"I don't know. Let me try standing on my hind legs. Ugh, that won't work. How about I stand here, and you climb up onto my back!"

"Oh, I don't know. That sounds scary, but I do love honey. Let's try it, new friend Bambi. Piglet, please keep watch and help where

you can.”

“Woah! Hold still, Bambi. Pooh, be careful up there. You're really high now!”

“Thank you, Piglet, but you do not need to fear. For I am hungry, and I do love honey.”

“Ah! Take it easy up there, Pooh. You're getting—ugh—heavy.”

“I'm sorry, friend Bambi. Ooh, hold still, I've got it—woah! —”

“Hey Eeyore! When did you get here?”

“About five minutes ago... thanks for noticing me.”

“Eeyore, look out!”

Maintaining his circular patrol far above the treetops, Tryggvi eyed the miniscule creatures quickly scurrying about the ground below. He immediately feared that they had spotted him high above their heads, but from what he could tell, they ran about in erratic circles with seemingly no direction or purpose. They weren't running away from him... they were simply running.

Straining his eyes, he zoomed in closer and noticed something odd about the donkey. There, atop his head, was a beehive. It must have fallen from one of the higher limbs and crashed down to slam onto the unsuspecting being. Tryggvi could see the delicious honey oozing from cracks in the hive, dripping down the side of the donkey's head and gluing itself to the being's black hair. A swarm of bees were flittering to-and-fro, diving toward the grey creature in a near continuous swarm of angry stings.

Licking his lips, he leaned forward, picking up speed as he tucked his wings closer to his body. The green rocket of a dragon plummeted toward the clearing below, its unsuspecting residents oblivious to the intruder rapidly approaching above their heads. Pitching his body around an outcropping of branches in the way from a massive pine tree, he corkscrewed his body around the adjacent copse and brought himself mere feet from the forest floor.

Opening his maw, his gleaming white teeth shined in the afternoon sunlight, hinting at their intended usage in the next few moments. Lining up on the bear, he belched out a burst of flame that arced gently up and down toward the spot where he anticipated the squat being to move to by the time that the plasma touched down. He watched in frustration as the bear zig-zagged out the way, seemingly oblivious to his attack and still battling the cluster of irate yellow and black defenders of the crumpled hive still stuck to the donkey's head.

Tryggvi plowed onward, a blur blasting through their group. Reaching out with his claws, he swung into the melee as he passed and banked up and around to the left, bringing himself around for another attack run. Looking down to his left hand, he grinned in anticipation as he saw the little pink piglet squirming to escape. Opening his mouth, he flicked the creature up and into the awaiting rows of razor sharp teeth and closed his eyes as he savored the taste of the sweet morsel upon his tongue. Circling the tops of the trees, he felt himself slip sideways as the blustery winds rocked his wings back and forth.

Squaring up for the attack, he pumped his wings and dove toward the ground once more, barreling straight into the formation of the animals below. They were scrambling about the edge of the trees, simultaneously trying to look for him in the cloud-laden sky above while also freeing their clumsy friend of the beehive. Closing the gap, he warmed his promethium glands and opening his jaw once more, letting three rapid bursts rocket forward to his awaiting entrees. Chasing the fireballs forward, he reeled in delight as he watched both the deer and donkey took the brunt of the fire on their sides, sending them off and over the edge of the hill. Their charred bodies bounced up and down the grassy embankment coming to a rest several wingspans away.

Tryggvi alighted on the warm grass and skidded to a halt. Eying the smoldering gray and brown bodies of his latest kills, he turned his attention back to the yellow blob scurrying away toward the tree line. Hunkering down, he sprung his legs up and forward, launching himself toward the creature. In three quick bounds, he put himself to the side and just passed where the bear would appear momentarily after rounding a nearby tree and turned in a powerful arc to whip his tail around. Completing the circuit and could just see the yellow fur emerge from the blind spot as it ran straight into his awaiting trap.

His tail met up with the small being, and upon connecting, launched the creature out of the trees and back into the middle of the field. Pivoting himself around the trees, Tryggvi playfully jumped back into the green circle, excited to inspect his kills.

Looking up, he saw the bear still falling to the ground, and just as it was about to connect, he belched out a stream of dragonfire to where he thought that it would be. The fire lurched forward, burning the air between the dragon and bear, and slammed into the falling body. If it wasn't dead already, it was now. Running forward, Tryggvi excitedly approached his three little meals, giddy with excitement. It had been so long since he had such an easy hunt followed by a diverse assortment of meats. Circling the group of creatures, he pawed them together into a single pile and curled himself around the bounty. Settling into the warm embrace of the sun-killed grasses and wildflowers, he arched his head upward, made his selection, and lunged downward to begin his feast.

A HAIKU

Tooth and claw flash white,
Dragons fight for dominance.
Skies cry out in pain.

THE GREEN RELIC

Draining the last of the iced coffee from the sweating cup, Liam Tryggvison closed his eyes and felt the caffeine rush through the veins of his tired body. He had been at it for hours, having only taken a short break to place an order for supper. Leaning back in the wooden chair and running his fingers through his dirty blonde hair, he looked around the library he had called home for the past week.

The room was, to put it simply, magnificent. Surrounded by high walls of massive, layered stones forming the foundation of the tower above, the library felt like it was lifted out of an Arthurian legend and dropped smack in the center of Worcester. How many people drove by this location every day, oblivious to the wonder that sat several stories below their feet? Dozens of handcrafted wooden bookshelves lined the walls, holding countless volumes of ancient lore. If you needed to know the lineage of a royal family, the origins of a particular dragon species, or the weaponry used at any battle from antiquity, there was a tome waiting for you on one of these shelves. And, if you needed to know something more recent, there was a strong Wi-Fi connection linked to the outside world. The Order of Draco was a civilized, up-to-date organization, after all.

Letting his eyes drift back to the table before him, he felt the blood pressure spike within his veins. Having nothing to do with the fresh intake of coffee, the shot of anxiety came from the condensation ring left on the cover of a nearby book by his cup of iced coffee.

"Oh crap!" Liam muttered, moving the now-empty vessel down to the stone floor. Frantically searching for a napkin, he took the edge of his t-shirt and dried the ring on the table, doing likewise to the cover of the victimized book. Holding the tome closer to this face for careful inspection, he blew a stream of air at the fading ring, desperately hoping that it wouldn't leave a permanent reminder of his negligence.

"What in Thor's name are you doing, Liam?"

Glancing up, Liam sheepishly placed the book back down on the tabletop while doing his best not to look guilty. "Ah, nothing! What are you doing, Lorenzo?"

Lorenzo Breno, the esteemed armorsmith for The Order of Draco, stood before him, staring in disgust. "Please tell me that you were not using the *Eiríks Saga Rauða* as a coaster for your rubbish American coffee."

"Um," Liam paused, knowing that he had been caught. "Yes, yes I was. But I didn't mean to! I was completely engrossed in this passage and forgot what I was doing. I'm sorry." Looking down at the now dried surface, he proudly held it aloft for Lorenzo to examine. "Look! It's dry."

Smiling proudly like an idiot and thinking that he had possibly diffused the situation, Liam turned his head as a knock came from the door. A short red-haired woman entered carrying a large brown paper bag.

"Excuse me, Liam and Lorenzo. Sorry for the intrusion. I have a delivery here for you." She paused, staring down at the bag in her hand with excitement. "Is this what I think it is?"

"Yes, yes, come in!" Liam excitedly proclaimed, trying to keep his voice low while ushering the woman over. "Thank you, Gena. Did Lady Luce see you? She'd kill me if she knew that this was in here."

Smirking, it was clear that Gena understood and had been successful in her subterfuge. "This isn't my first rodeo, Liam. No, I accomplished my covert mission."

"Would someone care to include me in whatever shadowy shenanigans you two are up to now?" Lorenzo asked, sniffing the air. "And what is that smell? Is that..."

"B.T.'s!" Gena exclaimed, opening the bag in her hands. "They do delivery now?"

Embarrassed to be found out and a little annoyed that he'd now have to share his bounty, Liam sighed. "Yes, yes... grab a plate. But don't tell anyone else!"

"You cannot eat BBQ in here, Liam!" Lorenzo muttered. "Why do I always feel like I'm the only adult in this place? There are tomes in here older than this country itself. There are original texts carried over by the earliest voyagers from the Nordic homelands. There's a treatise in that cabinet containing handwritten notes from Brynjar Magnusson himself. You cannot... cannot... are those beef short ribs?"

"Yes, and you can have one if you stop berating me. I'm well aware that I shouldn't have this in here. Please help me put these books away and we can have lunch while I tell you about my plan."

Twenty minutes later, the three members of The Order sat around the table with hands resting on their full bellies. Gena pushed her plate away, not wanting to see another ounce of food for fear of being sick.

"That was so good," she muttered, wiping Memphis sauce from the corner of her mouth. "Thank you for lunch, Liam. I'd love to stay, but I can't keep smelling that without wanting to eat more. Besides, Lucy probably needs me by now, and I don't want to be scarce when she comes calling." Pushing her chair out, she grabbed her sauce-covered mess and walked it out, heading towards the kitchen to clean up.

"So, Liam, what's your plan? Have you located another dragon? Are we heading to Greylock to help rebuild their tower? Or are we off to battle another insane dragon born from a deposed colonel?"

"Funny," Liam deadpanned, "but none of the above."

Rising from his chair while cleaning his fingers with a moist towelette, he turned to the stack of books and brought one back to the table. He smiled as he saw Lorenzo hastily wiping the table down and then drying it with a napkin. The man loved his ancient books and must have hated putting up with Liam and his borderline careless ways. Placing the aforementioned tome in front of the other man, he spun it around and opened it to where Liam had previously stuck a bookmark.

"This, my friend, is a later tale found only in our copy of *The Saga of Erik the Red*," Liam began. "It details an expedition led by Thorkell, one of Lief Erikson's children. The passage contains information regarding an exploratory venture into the Green Mountains of Vermont, where they searched for a dragon. It had been terrorizing the area, killing members of local villages and robbing them of precious metals, weapons, and other shiny valuables that dragons are partial to hoarding. The treatise doesn't provide much detail beyond that, only that the dragon was killed, the treasure was mostly returned to the respective villages, and that one of my ancestors was involved in the mission."

"So, where does The Order of Draco come in?" Lorenzo asked.

"Well, a few pages into the story, we see a footnote pointing to a journal kept by a friend of my ancestor. It mentions that during the journey into the cave, they ran into some trouble along the way, and this ancestor—one of Skùli Tryggvison's grandchildren—lost several pieces of kit and almost fell to his death."

"No way!" Lorenzo said, taking the text. "Does it say what he had lost?"

"Not in as much detail as you're hoping for, but take a look," Liam said, pointing to the part of the text where the story unfolded.

Eyeing the page, Lorenzo began to read out loud:

After slaying the green water dragon deep within the cavern system, we found ourselves climbing a steep chasm wall leading up from the river, where the battle commenced. Halfway up the rock, Ólafur Tryggvison slipped from his rope and fell into the dark waters below. Two of our men needed to restrain and raise him by ropes, not because of injury, but due to his fury at losing several pieces of gear. He reportedly lost a dagger passed down through his family, a sizeable quantity of gold coins, and a helmet rumored to be impervious to fire. I denied his request to go back to search for them due to our having run out of food and clean water and because several members of our party required healing. Ólafur has not spoken to me in several days now, but I have hopes that he'll come around.

"Huh," Lorenzo muttered.

"So, I think that I may be able to expand the Tryggvison Legacy a little. I have my leather cuirass, bracers, and greaves, as well as the steel pauldrons and gorget, but I lack a proper helm. I'm wondering if a Tryggvison-made helmet is lying in wait deep within that cave, destined to be rediscovered by my bloodline." After a moment's pause, he continued. "Are you thinking what I'm thinking?"

"I'm thinking that we're going to Vermont," Lorenzo replied.

"Road trip!" Liam shouted. "Pack your bags. I'll go round up Katerina and Alex."

One week later, the crew was on their way northwest to Weybridge, Vermont. From what they could tell, the mission to slay the dragon and return their lost treasures had led the adventurers to a cavern located in a heavily wooded area just north of modern-day Middlebury. Using maps found online from a regional cave exploration grotto, the four members easily pinpointed their target location.

After pulling off Route 23 and making their way down some dirt roads leading towards the state park, they parked near a farm and made their way through an open field.

"Are we there yet?" Katerina quipped from the back of the pack.

"We just started walking," Liam retorted. "It's not that far. Look, the cave should be just up there inside the tree line."

"Yeah, easy for you to say," she countered. "You're not the one carrying all of the climbing gear. You only have that map to worry about."

"And my sword!" Liam fired back, smirking. He knew that she was right. As the resident armorer at their headquarters, Katerina Paquinova had spent a lifetime hammering countless pieces of steel plate and other custom items for her clients. One of whom was Liam, who was always finding new ways to damage his and need extensive repairs. She was naturally the strongest of their crew and often volunteered, to her regret, to lug heavier items on such trips.

"I'll take you to Woodchuck after," Liam called back, knowing that it would cheer her up. "Drinks on me?"

"Deal."

With their future drink plans settled, they worked their way into the tree line and swiftly found the mouth of the cavern. The ragged black hole plunged deep into the hillside, dropping down and out of sight within thirty feet of the entrance. Donning their gear and checking each other for readiness, they carefully made their way into the darkness with Liam in the lead.

Following the path inside, they slowly proceeded down and to the right as they worked their way through the blackness that can only be found deep beneath the earth. It would normally be clearer earlier in the year, but the local bat population must have just woken from their winter hibernation and disturbed the settled dust within the long winding tunnel. They couldn't see any bats hanging from the ceiling, but the piles of guano spotting the ground all around them indicated that they had been there until recently.

Coming to a stop at a junction in the winding tunnel system, Liam shot up his right arm with a clenched fist. The three members behind slowed to a halt and pointed their headlamps in his direction.

"What do you see, Liam?" Katerina whispered.

"We've reached a fork in the road," Liam replied, pulling his laminated map out of a cargo pocket on his coveralls. "If our interpretation of the journal is correct, the men traveled this way," Liam said, pointing off to the left.

"How far from here until we get to our target?" Alex asked. "I don't remember the journal providing many details about distance, just their findings and events."

"No clue, unfortunately," Liam conceded as he resumed walking. He wanted to be annoyed by the lack of information found within his family's journals, but they were writings from over a thousand years ago. The fact that he had access to the writings at all was amazing and he should count it as a blessing. "But from what I read, it didn't sound like they had traveled very long. I assume that we'll find the drop sooner rather than…"

Liam's foot shot out into the empty air instead of landing on hard stone as expected. He started to fall forward when he felt a hand shoot out and grab him by the harness.

"Waahh!"

"Hang on!" Lorenzo yelled from behind him. "Alex, grab my harness and pull us up!"

Alex Oakenstaff, one of the premier ancient combat experts in the U.S. and arguably the western hemisphere, was easily capable of singlehandedly wrenching the weight of both men from the grasp of the gravitational pull from deep within the earth. Liam felt himself being yanked up and graciously dropped onto the rocky edge of the cliff. He didn't move until his chest stopped heaving, staring at the illuminated circle of the ceiling above. Sitting up a few minutes later, he scrambled further from the edge and turned to thankfully see that he wasn't the only one scared by their shared experience.

"I think that we found the drop-off," Alex stated, a hint of mirth filling the quiet void surrounding them.

"Thanks, bud," Liam quipped. "Let's check our gear and get the ropes set up. Looks like we found our way down."

Twenty minutes later, after securing the harnesses and anchoring two sets of rappelling ropes to several sturdy-looking stalagmites, the quartet was ready to descend into the darkness.

Taking the lead, Liam clipped himself onto the rope using a self-braking descender. Moving his back-mounted scabbard to accommodate the full-body climbing harness, he adjusted his kit until things felt balanced and comfortable. He'd prefer to wear a small competition harness, but they opted for the larger option in case one of them needed to be pulled out. Making his way toward the edge of the rock, he was about to lean back when the peanut gallery spoke up.

"Do you really need to bring your sword?" Katerina questioned, her tone drier than desert sand.

Liam feigned personal insult. "Leave my sword? Leave Liberator behind for anyone to steal? How dare you?!"

Katerina stared back at him, wordless. Liam was a terrible actor and couldn't hold it in any longer. He finally broke and smirked.

"Okay, you're right," he conceded. "I probably didn't need to bring Liberator. I just don't have many reasons nowadays, and... and... it just feels cool to have it on my back, that's all."

"Well, as long as you're being honest," she replied. "It's not worth the time to remove the sword now that you're already in your gear, so you might as well leave it on. Besides, we might need to open some envelopes down there or something."

"Alright, let's get to work," Liam said, sticking his tongue out at her. "I'll go down first. If things look safe, Katerina will rappel down the second line to join me. Once we reach the bottom, we'll call up. Then Lorenzo and Alex will join us. Agreed?"

A trio of nods acknowledged his plan. His responding nod sealed the deal. Repositioning himself along the edge of the drop-off, he shifted his weight from foot to foot and reaffirmed his bearings. He was ready.

"On belay?"

"Belay on," Lorenzo replied.

"Rappelling," Liam stated. Leaning back, he smoothly walked himself down the vertical face into the unknown.

Panning side to side, he let the light from his helmet play across the features around him. While a hiker by nature, he was no stranger to cave exploration. The darkness and rock closing in around him didn't bother him that much anymore. What did scare him was what may lie just beyond the darkness. He had learned firsthand that monsters really did exist.

As he continued to descend, he could hear the calming trickles and gurgles of their destination somewhere down below. Looking down, he frowned. His light failed to penetrate the darkness and robbed him of the chance to spot the elusive underground river. Looking around and not seeing anything of concern, he let the gear take his weight and stood on a rocky outcropping to rest.

"Katerina!"

"Liam!" she called back. "You good?"

"Yep," he replied. "I think that I'm about halfway to the bottom. You might as well begin your descent."

"On my way!"

A moment later, he could see the rope next to him begin to flap about, slapping the rock and waving out in the distance. Preceded by a gentle shower of fine sand and pebbles, he heard hot rope rushing through a belay device followed by the whooping of someone having far too much fun.

"Woo!" Katerina yelped as she brought herself to a hard stop adjacent to Liam. "Woah, that was a nice drop."

"Heh, I'm glad that you had fun," Liam deadpanned. "As long as you didn't rip that stalagmite out of the floor up there, you should be fine. Lorenzo is probably going nuts checking over the knots to see if you jostled anything loose."

Descending together, it only took another minute of relatively slow travel to get their boots wet. Katerina, trying to beat Liam in a very one-sided race to the bottom, splashed down first and victoriously announced it to her rappelling partner.

From their vantage point, they couldn't see much of anything. The walls of the cave rose vertically from the water and disappeared into the inky black above. The river was no more than ten feet wide where they stood, and from what he could tell, fluctuated between five to fifteen feet as far as his light would travel in either direction. Looking down into the clear yet turbulent water yielded no additional information.

Motioning to Kat, the two pulled up their ropes until they were just out of the water. They weren't wearing waterproof gear and had nothing to gain by slowly catching hypothermia in the bowels of the earth. Gripping the two-way clipped to the shoulder strap of his harness, he radioed back to the two men waiting above.

"Hey guys, we're at the bottom," Liam spoke into the mic. "Good thing, too, because we didn't have much line left on the ropes. Over."

"What do you see," Alex replied. "Anything neat? Over."

"Unfortunately, no," Liam said. "Would you run back and grab the scuba gear? At least one of us should go under and poke around. We're above a fairly shallow section, but it looks to drop down deeper on either side. Over."

"Roger. Give us a few minutes and we'll be down to join you. Over."

"Acknowledged. Over."

Clipping the radio onto its strap, Liam pushed off from the rock and allowed himself to swing back and forth across the chasm. Looking down at the water, he shined the light back and forth, trying to see if anything was visible through the frigid water. Not seeing anything of interest, he looked back up at Katerina and froze. Crawling along the rock wall just behind her was a dark green water dragon.

"KAT, DROP NOW!"

Turning to see what was coming, she already had her hand on the belay device and squeezed it hard. As she dropped into the churning waves below, a rush of flame shot through the space her body had occupied just a heartbeat earlier. The rope vaporized above her head, aiding in her descent and melting a few of the stickers on her helmet.

Liam pushed off the chasm wall and launched himself through the air. Holding the rope with his left while reaching for his sword with his right, he swung towards the dragon ready to strike. Another blast left the gaping maw of the small dragon, heading his way. Bringing the sword around into a defensive position, Liam blocked the shot and smiled with glee as Liberator absorbed the energy.

Finishing the swing across the void with his sword shimmering pulses of energy from the crossguard to the tip, he hit the other side of the chasm and grabbed onto a protrusion. Feeling the sword hum with a vibrant life not present a moment ago, he needed to act soon before the built-up potential found its own way out.

"Who are you?" he screamed at the dragon. He knew that it was either a primal or a sapient dragon, and there was only one way to find out. To his delight, the dragon paused. "You understand me, correct?"

A perplexed look flushed the face of the newcomer. From what Liam could tell, the creature must be a recently hatched whelp, no bigger than a baby horse. Its wings were still tiny and cute, and most likely incapable of sustaining flight. That explained why the dragon was climbing along the walls instead of soaring through the air above.

The dragon, seemingly unsure what to make of him, continued to stare back at him. Against his better judgement and relying on the rope from above to hold his weight, Liam slowly moved along the wall to close the gap between him and the creature. He did keep the river between them; he wasn't an idiot. Maintaining eye contact with the whelp, he tried to dispel any tension in his stance or appearance. Scaring the young being any more than he already had was the last thing that he wanted to do. Reaching the point where he was directly across from the water dragon, he leaned out over the water to get a better look and show the creature that he wasn't afraid. After a moment's pause, to his delight, the dragon mimicked his action and seemed to reach out to him, as well.

Until the voice crackled from his radio. "LIAM! We're back. What's your status? Over."

The dragon roared and bared its teeth at Liam, crouching back along the length of the wall. Its wings arched outward and body lowered to the rocky face of the chasm wall, it slowly retreated.

"Alex!" Liam whispered into the mic. "Keep quiet, we're okay!"

"What? I can't make out your words. Over."

The creature's anger exploded. The green dragon launched a fireball straight up the cliff face toward the commotion above. Before it could find its target, another fusillade was flying in Liam's direction. He barely had time to swing the sword back up into position to absorb the flames when he felt himself lurch away from the rock and down into the river. Looking up, he could see the singed end of his rope fluttering down after him as they both plunged into the frigid water below.

Landing hard on the rocks just below the river's surface, he managed to keep his wits about him despite the crunching sensation coming from his left knee. Holding the sword above water, he traced the motion of the dragon and unleashed the pent-up energy.

"I'm sorry, buddy," he muttered as a flash of blue light leapt from the tip of Liberator. The blast hit the chasm wall adjacent to the dragon's chest, launching the latter amidst of shower of rubble into the water a few yards upriver.

"Liam, no!" Katerina cried out.

Sword extended and trying his best to ignore the intense heat rushing through his leg with each agonizing step, Liam waded through the river towards where he saw the dragon plunge below the surface. Stubbing his toe on something, he looked down to see a random mixture of dull green and reflective black objects. Sidestepping them, he made his way to the unmoving creature below.

Gently poking its tail through the icy waves with the tip of his sword, he failed to see a reaction come from the being. Trying to ignore the impulse coming from his gut, he decided to act on it before his brain told him otherwise. Quickly returning Liberator to his back and gritting his teeth, he reached into the water and felt around for something substantial to grab a hold of. Dropping to one knee, he powered himself and the bundle of scales, claws, and wings upward into the breathable air.

"Kat, you okay?"

"Yeah," she stammered. "But... is he... did you...?"

"No, I don't think so, thankfully," he replied. "I've got him, for now. Would you call the lads above for some fresh ropes, and grab that stuff down by your feet? I think that we hit the jackpot today."

Several days later, the four exhausted, but healthy members of The Order of Draco sat around the kitchen table back in Worcester. With his leg propped up on an empty chair next to him, Liam did his best to keep his braced knee comfortable. While the partially torn PCL made extraction from the cave a little more difficult, it had done nothing to slow him down during their morning's activities.

Arrayed before them sat the spoils of their expedition. The members had spent the past two days and nights delicately cleaning, analyzing, and photographing the items found in the subterranean river. They had finally finished early this morning and were now passing them back and forth with white gloves, gently inspecting each other's work with the attention and excitement of museum caretakers. There were several ancient coins, a dagger, a small camp axe, and as dreamt of, a glittering Gjermundbu-style helmet.

"Lorenzo, this is amazing," Liam said, while holding the helm between his hands. "This looked like nothing more than a hunk of green rock just two days ago. I thought that it was an old copper bowl when we pulled it from the water. What did you do?"

"Ooh! Can I tell him?"

Lorenzo sighed, but acquiesced. "By all means, Katerina. It was your idea which brought this to light, after all."

"Yay!" The woman danced in her chair. "So, when we first pulled it out of the river, it was all crusty and gross. I'm not sure if you got a good look at it with your busted knee and all. But, as you said, it just looked like a misshapen bowl. From what we know, I figured that any helm which we would have found down there would either be bronze, steel, or something in between. If it was the former, the whole thing may have been green and corroded, and possibly disappeared by now. If it was steel, it would have probably rusted and disintegrated due to oxygen being plentiful in the water. Plus, it'd be red." She stopped to take a deep breath, the excitement pouring out of her words and facial expressions. "But! Based on how it looked, I figured that it might have originally been a copper-plated steel helm. The text that you discovered wasn't clear on the matter, but it was worth the shot."

Lorenzo raised his hand to speak, but Kat wasn't giving up her soapbox just yet. The stodgy old blacksmith always got to tell cool metallurgical stories, but this one was hers.

"As you could see from before," she said, while sliding one of the initial photographs of the helm across the table for the others to see, "the cuprous chloride in the copper plating reacted with the water and oxygen to produce hydrochloric acid which ate away at the plating over a millennia. There were a few baren spots on the inside of the helm where the plating must have been thinner, hence the rust on the inside."

Liam turned the helm over and around to inspect the area in question.

"So, between a little salt and vinegar scrub and an overnight soak in an electrolysis bath, we were able to remove all of the corroded copper and bring it back to the inner steel."

"Which led us," Lorenzo began, looking to seize an opportunity in the momentary silence, "to find this." He leaned forward to point to an area on the back of the helm where a series of runes were engraved into the steel.

"What does it say?" Liam asked, his voice quieting to a near whisper.

"That, my friend, is Old Norse for Tryggvison," Lorenzo replied, beaming.

Later that night, Liam sat on a bench outside of a cell deep within the tower's foundation. He stared longingly at the small creature sleeping in a pile of hay behind the cold iron bars. The same creature which had tried to kill him just a few days ago.

"What will you do with her?" he asked the woman standing in the open doorway. He had heard her footsteps approach but didn't need to look up to know who it was. "Will she need to remain locked up like this?"

"We're not sure," Gena replied. "It's pretty much up to her now. If she's indeed a sapient dragon and not a primal, then we should be able to communicate with her once she regains consciousness. Your redirected fireblast packed a wallop and she's been in and out of it ever since. We've given her water and nutritional injections to maintain her vitals, but she needs to make the next move."

"Thank you for all that you've done," Liam said. "I'm sorry to bring her back here, you know, if something bad happens, but I didn't know what else to do. I didn't want to put you, Lucy, and the rest of The Order in danger, but I just couldn't leave her like that."

"You did the right thing, Liam. This isn't our first rescued dragon," Gena said. "Come, let's head back upstairs. From what I've heard, you have a new helm to try on."

INVASION

For what felt like the hundredth time that morning, Odagda stared out the window of the keep to the volcano across the plains. Rising high above the neighboring lands, the ominous mountain continued to release a small yet steady trail of wispy smoke to the passing winds. The looming mass of land had sat there watching and waiting since long before his earliest known ancestors came to live on this rock. It was an ever-present object seen in the backdrop of all-important matters in their culture. Quiet and innocent yet exhibiting just enough hint of its potential power to leave even the smartest academic wary of its future. The volcano had not properly erupted in almost a decade and was expected to deliver a walloping deluge to the plains below any day now. Well, that's at least what his lead scientist had been claiming.

Sighing, he turned his attention back to the speaker standing before him. He had been sitting upon his throne for nearly four hours now listening to countless reports coming in from his council. Each report detailed yet another dismal status update of his kingdom and drove him further into despair. While he thought of himself as a resourceful and clever being, he had reached the point of giving up and breaking the bad news to his people: they were all going to starve to death.

"I'm sorry, sir, are you alright?"

Snapping out of it, he quickly swung his massive head around toward the voice and focused his eyes upon the younger dragon. Thougus, the governor of the capital city of Calderopolis, the seat of

Odagda's power, deserved far more respect than he was currently receiving from his lordship.

"Yes, yes. My humblest apologies, Governor Thougus," Odagda began. "My mind is elsewhere, and I'm having a hard time staying focused on the matter at hand."

"Sir, we can do this another time, if you prefer," the governor offered kindly. The look on his face said otherwise.

"No, please, continue," Odagda said softly. "You will have my full attention; I promise."

And so, the governor picked back up where he had left off and proceeded through his report. He rattled off inventory levels, daily consumption of necessary goods, the current death toll for the day, weather forecasts, and poll data from the constituents. The news was grave and the emotions dire. He couldn't recall a time in his life when things had seemed so grim.

Odagda, leader of the Dragons of Mars, had spent his entire life watching his father and his father before him guide their race to prosperity. The population of the planet had exploded as technology developed, and in turn, their overall livelihood had improved and the dragons in general were happy. Things had been perfect.

Until they weren't.

Several years ago, rumors began to trickle in from the outlying provinces that food supplies were dwindling. The dragons of those areas needed to import increasingly larger quantities of food from the main principalities to supplement their own locally produced goods and wares. What had once been self-sufficient populations were now hungry and needy creatures begging and pleading for basic necessities. For a noble being such as a dragon of their race, the act was an embarrassment and brought shame to their clans. But it had become an unfortunate and unavoidable necessity. There were simply too many mouths to feed and not enough sustainable sources of nourishment. In the matter of several millennia, they had gone from a small population on a new planet amidst a lush rainforest to an overpopulated cluster of angry and hungry dragons living in quarters too dense for their massive bodies.

Forcing his eyes to come back into focus, he saw the room and dragon before him go from a gentle blur to a crisp image once again. He almost missed it, but he could see the look of recognition on the other dragon's face as Thougus realized he had lost his leader once more. The dragon, being far too kind, did not miss a beat and continued onward with his updates. As he reached the end of his report, Odagda thanked him for his hard work, promised to have some answers shortly, and wished him well.

And so, his day went by. One dragon would leave as another entered and began his or her respective news updates. While each dragon represented a different division of labor or section of their society, the tone of their delivered information was the same. Things were going from bad to worse with little to no clear answer on how to solve their problems. Each respective leader had good ideas on how to mitigate their issues, but no one could think of a way to completely remedy the situation. One after another, they turned to their leader for guidance and support.

As the last dragon left the throne room for the evening, Odagda slowly rose from his modest seat and winced. He hadn't moved his muscles in hours, and they protested each step down the raised dais to the stone floor below. He flexed his limbs and stretched out his mighty wings to their full breadth, each wingtip almost touching the opposing wall. He had lived a good, long life here on Mars and his strong, muscular body showed it. Looking to the horizontal rays of sunlight streaking through the windows, he realized just how late it was and that he hadn't seen his wife all day. If he was lucky, there may even be supper left waiting for him at home.

With his tail sliding on the dry stone behind him, he rounded the corner into the doorway of his personal chambers which he shared with his queen, Frigghus. Shuffling through the spacious, yet spartanly decorated entryway, he made his way through their living quarters until he reached their dining room. Just as he entered, the love of his life came through the door from the kitchen carrying a small platter of meats, cheeses, and other basic foodstuffs.

"Odagda, my love, you're home!" his wife said, a smile quickly spreading across her face. "I was beginning to think that I'd need to bring your food out to you in the chamber."

Despite the long hours and taxing strain on his mind and body, after even the worst of days, the sight of her razor-sharp teeth gleaming out of her beautiful smile could make him bounce back to his usually happy self.

"Almost, almost," he said, chuckling. "But not today. If there's one thing that this plight has taught me, it's to focus on that which matters most."

Knowing his meaning, her smile grew by several more inches across her scaly visage. After all these long years of courtship and marriage, he still knew how to charm her.

"Are you hungry?" she asked, moving towards their humble kitchen. "I admittedly went ahead and ate without you, but I saved a good portion of the meal and can warm it up for you."

"Yes, my love, and thank you for saving me some," he replied. "What did you make?"

Bending low to place the tray of food over a griddle in the fireplace, she tossed a few pieces of wood underneath and backed up. Puffing her lungs, she belched out a slow and gentle stream of fire at the small stack of tinder under the griddle and quickly ignited it. Satisfied with her work, she stood up to her full height and answered, "A few grilled deer flanks and some mushrooms." Her shoulders drooped. "Nothing fancy, but it's the best that we have left."

Swinging his bulk around the island in their spacious yet modestly appointed kitchen, he put his arms around his wife and pulled her in for a warm embrace. "This will be wonderful; I can taste it already. Times are tough and we must lead by example. If the people are eating basic foodstuffs, then so shall we."

She smiled back up at him and rested her jaw upon his shoulder, just above his wings.

"Come, let's sit down by the window while the food warms up. I want to hear about your day."

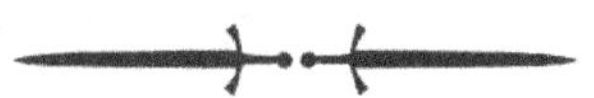

"Enjoy your meal!"

"Have a nice supper!"

"Here's your allotment, sir. Say 'hi' to your clutch for me!"

"Well, I guess I can give you a tiny extra scoop. But don't tell anyone!"

For hours on end, the dragon behind the soup counter in the food distribution center doled out the regrettably small rations to the hungry masses. She worked tirelessly to find new foodstuffs for her fellow dragons and developed ingenious ways to stretch out each meal to fill the empty bellies of those around her. It was often a thankless job in this difficult time, but she accepted the challenge and relished the opportunity to do her part.

In previous years, her job was easy and almost boring at times. The population was low, and food was aplenty. Shipments would come in from the hunters and gatherers, she'd process the goods into delicious meals, dragons would come in, and dragons would go home. The average dragon had taken it for granted that food would always be there just waiting for them and never had to think about when their next meal would arrive. Few would say 'thank you' and most didn't give her the time of day. Most would just walk up to the counter, sniff the simmering stews and soups available at her buffet, take what they wanted, and move on. It was a rarity when another dragon actually looked her in the eye and acknowledged her presence.

And then one day it all changed. Nobody noticed the developments immediately and they certainly didn't happen overnight. Starting slowly, and then very, very quickly, the food supplies dwindled to half, then a quarter, down to just mere scraps with each passing day. What had once been a bountiful harvest awaiting the influx of hungry beings become a shadow of its former self.

Meat became scarce and she was forced to increase her usage of fruits and vegetables to offset the void while filling the empty stomachs of her patrons. Different grains, roots, and tubers which had once been seen as side dishes and garnishes were now deemed as main entrees. She had quickly learned how to season and prepare new dishes in unusual ways to keep the masses fed and satisfied. Some dragons scoffed at her new creations, but most came around as their standards lowered or evolved to the new challenges. As dragons become more desperate to feed themselves and their families, their appreciation for her efforts and product surprisingly increased. She now had dragons recognize her on the streets after hours, thank her for her continued work, and praise her for keeping their bellies full and hunger low. In the midst of all the troubling times and lowered spirits, she continued to smile as she worked knowing that her importance to the community, even if just the perception of it, had improved. If that was the only silver lining out of all of this, it was enough to encourage her to keep going and help her fellow dragons.

Checking the levels of the vats before her, she noticed that the weasel and onion stew was almost to the bottom. Carefully swinging her massive tail around as she spun her body, she managed not to knock anything over in the cramped cooking space as she turned to the stove on the back counter and retrieved a large ladle to refill the pot. Grabbing the utensil from the drying rack with her clawed hands, she reflexively dropped to the floor as a sharp crash echoed across the dining hall. Her muscles tensed, she slowly rose on her hands and knees and looked around the corner of her counter.

Several wingspans away, a large turquoise dragon had clearly just been thrown backwards by a snarling maroon being at least half again his size. The former—while most likely outmatched in a one-on-one fight—did not appear to be backing down and was standing his ground before the aggressor. Looking behind the smaller one, the vendor noticed that the turquoise had thrown out his wings and was shielding two small whelps.

"You spilled my stew!" the larger dragon roared in anger, his eyes aflame as he stared down at his opposer. "Give me all three of your bowls now for compensation!"

Puffing out his chest, the smaller of the two stared back in defiance and growled his reply. "I said that I was sorry for bumping into you and spilling your bowl. You can have mine for repayment of my clumsiness, but let the young ones eat theirs."

"Those whelps must learn respect for their elders," the maroon bellowed. "And you alone are obviously not able to teach them right from wrong. This lesson will teach them not to be like their foolish father."

"Please, just take my bowl and go back to your seat. I said that I was sorry. Leave them out of it."

The larger dragon stretched out his impressive wings and stood up to his full height. "Give me all of your food now, or I will eat you instead!". Reaching out, the dragon grabbed their table and flung it to the side, crashing violently into a nearby table. The impact scattered food and drinks across the scales of the unsuspecting dragons, only amplifying the fervor already building in the dining area.

"Kids, run!"

"ENOUGH!" a voice boomed from high above. Turning their heads to the sky to find the source of the bellow, the diners found themselves cast in a faint shadow as a large object momentarily blotted out the afternoon sunlight. Before the soundwaves of the commanding word had finished echoing between the walls of the nearby buildings, an immense being crashed down into the middle of the throng of dragons.

Tables and chairs clattered to the side as the being slammed into the paving stones. A rush of dust and splinters blasted outward from the impact crater his landing left behind, briefly obscuring the vision of the still-shocked vendor and her customers.

Staring through the hazy air, she could just make out the hulk of Toudall, the Chief of Security for all of Calderopolis. She could see the dragon scanning the crowd, quickly taking in the scene and gathering intelligence in one focused pass.

Years of experience maintaining peace in his city and a keen understanding of the social and political issues at hand, helped the elder dragon observe the situation and ascertain his next steps. Reaching a clawed hand out on the end of an arm bristling with muscular strength, he grabbed the bullying dragon by the neck, pumped his wings once while pushing off with his hindlegs, and launched the pair into the sky above.

Craning her head out from under the awning over her station, she tried to watch the duo ascend above the pavilion. She could just make out the sight of their tails and wingtips whipping through the hazy afternoon air before they disappeared beyond the edges of the taller buildings. Turning back to her rear counter, she hefted the vat of stew and carried it out to the silent crowd. Shock had taken hold of many, and an equal number barely noticed that their food had been spilled in the brief conflict, robbing them of their much-needed nutrients. Setting to work, she helped the mass of hungry dragons right their tables and chairs, retrieve their spilled bowls, and refilled those who needed it. She'd find a way to stretch this meal out. No dragon would go hungry on her watch.

A gout of fire shot across the wide expanse of the council chamber, quickly following in the wake of a bellowing voice echoing around the hallowed walls of the ancient building.

"Order! Order!" the voice rang out in a commanding tone.

The crowd settled back down and took their seats. Whether they did so from the fire or shouting was to be debated.

Seeing the crowd remain surprisingly silent and attentive for the moment, Odagda took the opportunity to rise from his seat and address the congregation before more rumors and side conversations could fly from one side to the other once again. The dragons knew that something was wrong and demanded information from their leadership.

"Dragons!" their leader roared out to the masses. The dragons roared back in unison, the customary greeting and reply for a meeting of this kind. He could hear that many of the roars were polite and respectful, some carried a harsh undertone to them and had been ushered forth from angry maws. He'd need to choose his next few words carefully if he was to appease their concerns, guide them into a proactive path forward, and if he was lucky, leave this room with his tail and wings still attached.

"My fellow dragons, I hear you and sympathize with your worries," he began, slowly picking his way through the opening statement. He wasn't giving them good news and knew that he'd further anger many within the crowd. He wasn't really afraid for his life and knew that if he had to, he could take even a large clawful of them together in a fight. No, he was worried about fracturing the populace further with deeper cuts to their closely held beliefs. If he tore them apart and pushed these dragons away from the bargaining table so early on, then their entire race would be doomed from the start. "As many of you know, we are in a grave time and the outlook on the world is grim. Many of you are without food and water, and those who are lucky to have either, find it to be in short supply and at a great cost to your coffers.

"Our population has exploded, and the planet as a whole is incredibly vibrant with life. We have experienced many wonderful boons in our civilization, and I continue to be amazed by the ingenuity and work ethic of you and our fellow dragons. But it has come at a painful cost. As our numbers continue to steadily rise, we strip the land of the vital nutrients and generous resources which we have taken for granted for so long."

Odagda paused here as a few angry roars reverberated from several spots within the crowd. While all scientific thought and basic statistics pointed at this being a dragon-borne problem, it had become quite a political debate amongst his people as to the real culprit. Many wanted to take action now, or even years ago if they could turn back time, to fix the problem before it got worse. Others, however, said that these changes were natural and happened cyclically throughout their planet's lifetime. The difference in thought had created a rift in their society, with dragons on both extreme ends clawing at each other's throat over the issue. It was clear that policy change, thoughts, nor prayers would solve this issue.

"Our scholars and civic leaders have discussed at length what would happen when we ultimately grew too numerous but have always dismissed it as a far-off concern for another time and another generation." He paused here, wanting to let the next few words sink in with the minds of his fellow dragons. "Unfortunately, that time is now and the generation to solve this problem is our own."

Looking around the room, he took in the concerned faces of his friends and family. Some he had known for his entire life, while others were young and had only just begun to sample a taste of the joyful life that this planet had to offer... up until only a short time ago. He no longer felt sorry for the loss which he could potentially experience but pitied them for never having the chance to live the life which they had so well deserved. He may not have started this dilemma, but he surely had not done enough to prevent its progression. Panning the room with his tired eyes, he looked up and tried to connect with each and every soul in the chamber, both friend and foe alike.

Over the past several months, many of his kind had turned against him for his lack of effort to stymy the issues while an equal number had attacked him for being too harsh in his governance. No matter what he had done, he couldn't make all of the dragons happy. Frankly, it felt like he wasn't making any of them happy. Never before had he seen his fellow dragons so fundamentally divided, especially on something with such an obvious outcome. Their species would die without some form of intervention.

Sighing, he took a deep breath and resumed his address. "It is with heavy heart that I must admit to you that I alone do not know the correct path forward."

A crescendo of angry roars and horrified gasps echoed around the room as a flurry of exasperated conversations erupted throughout the crowd. Holding out his clawed hands, he gestured to them to remain calm and let him finish.

"However, I find myself surrounded by the brightest and most creative dragons to have ever lived on this planet. I am forming a special task group to work directly with me and the rest of the council over the next week to address our concerns. We will analyze the problems, both immediate and long-term, review all possible scenarios, and devise the most beneficial solution for the greater good of all dragonkind."

With the room suddenly awash in both roars and gouts of fire alike, Odagda bowed his head and strode through the rear exit. Whether from exhaustion, shame, or fear of his constituents' furious glares, he couldn't muster the courage to look them in the eyes as he departed the chamber. While he remained hopeful that his inner circle could work together and think of a solution to get their race out of their dire predicament, he was too much of a realist to know how bad the situation had become.

They needed an answer, and they needed it now.

Trailed by a long meandering path of two sets of footprints and lazily swirling tail marks through the sandy field, the two dragons made their way to the edge of the corral and leaned against the bright white painted wooden fence. If the dusty walk through the once vibrantly green fields of grasses and flowers hadn't made the troubles at hand obvious enough, the poor state of the herd solidified the situation for Odagda. Where there should have been a large herd of bovines casually grazing with their fellow cows, there was just a small gathering of a dozen famished creatures. Their hides were shrunken and clinging to their rib cages. The poor things hadn't seen a good meal in ages, and some appeared incapable of doing anything more than laying in the shade while hoping for the merciful embrace of death.

"Forsetius, I am so sorry," Odagda muttered. "Is it like this with your other herds?"

"This is all that's left of my herds," the dragon replied, his wing tips shaking despite the lack of breeze. The sound of embarrassment and frustration culminated in his next word, sounding both like an honorific and a sarcastic blow. "Sir."

Odagda nodded solemnly. He had known the farmer for many years now and was well aware that Forsetius's herd of cattle was the dragon's pride and joy in life. He had been world-renowned across all of Mars for having the finest animals under his care producing the finest tasting milk and meat. Restaurants, markets, and high-class clientele alike fought to be on a first name basis with him to source their tables with the best of the best. The dragon's current demeanor spoke volumes to the experiences which he had gone through over the past few months. No rain, no crops, no support of any kind from the markets, nor the government had brought him to his breaking point. His farm, his reputation, his livelihood... were gone.

Filling his lungs with the dusty air and slowly letting it out again, he finally spoke. "What can I do for you, Forsetius, my friend?"

Turning to his leader, and long-time friend, Forsetius replied quietly after a pause. "May I speak openly, sir?"

"You may always speak your mind with me, Forsetius."

The farmer gulped, looking side to side across his field. Content that no other dragons were near enough to overhear, he finally spoke.

"We're getting desperate, sir," Forsetius admitted. "We're low on food; water is scarce; and our sanity is balancing on the tip of a talon. We need help, Odagda. We common dragons down here on the ground have watched you and your family fly up to your lofty lair while we struggle to survive down in the dust."

Odagda winced at the out lash. It was hard for him to hear these words coming from his friend, but he couldn't deny any of it. While he considered himself a humble dragon who tried to live below his means, he knew damn well that he and his family had it better than most of his fellow dragons. He may not live in the gleaming ivory tower that Forsetius insinuated, but it wasn't dramatically far from the truth.

"I'm sorry, sir," Forsetius backpedaled, clearly seeing the look of pain on his friend's face. "I know that this isn't your fault, but you are our leader, and the people look to you for guidance and support. Something must be done, and it must be done now before it gets worse."

Promising to fix things quickly and bidding his friend farewell, Odagda pushed off from the parched ground and took to the sky. Purposely choosing a meandering path which took him over several of the adjacent farms, he toured the region as he flew home to get a better sense of the current state of his lands. It was bad, and far worse than he could have imagined. Banking gently with the breeze, he pointed himself back toward the center of the capital city and his home within.

He had work to do.

Two days later, Odagda found himself wing-to-wing with two dozen of his fellow dragons in one of the larger meeting rooms within his residence. While he normally would have tried to meet at one of the more formal governmental buildings, swarms of protesting dragons surrounding the downtown areas made it difficult to easily navigate the streets and sky lanes. While he wasn't wary of violence towards himself and his other leaders just yet, he was well aware that they were one more bad incident away from all out, general unrest among the populace. The dragons were on the verge of unleashing their pent up frustration among the populace. Best case scenario... it would boil over into some random riots around the city. Worst case? There would be a revolution and his head would wind up on a pike.

It was better to steer clear for the time being.

The assembled task force, the same one which he had promised his constituents several days earlier would quickly work together to solve their resource concerns and restore health and security to their race, had been together for over a day now and had seemingly accomplished nothing.

While the meeting had started with an enthusiastic and

promising attitude, it had quickly unraveled into a series of prolonged shouting matches. Not that he would ever disclose it to the public, but a few physical altercations had broken out amongst several of the more aggressive members of the team. Each dragon present meant well and had their best intentions in mind for their own respective field of expertise, but in the end, there was no single plan of attack that they could all agree upon.

As another tense discussion was well underway, Odagda sighed heavily, realizing the eventual outcome. Rising from his bench at the table, he stood to his impressive full height and stretched out his wings. The sudden gesture from their leader quickly quieted the group as they noticed his change of stature and looked to him for his anticipated words.

"Thank you," Odagda called out, putting as calm of a tone to his voice as he could possibly muster. He was frustrated with the lack of progress from among his team but couldn't let them see that. Besides, it wasn't entirely their fault. They didn't directly do anything wrong leading up to their current predicament. Centuries of regrettable decisions aimed to make their short-term lives better in lieu of a more difficult future had collectively led them down this path. They were all innocent and sadly, all equally guilty.

"It is clear that we are not going to come to a consensus today, nor any time in the near future, from what I'm hearing," their leader continued. "But I thank you all for your hard work over the past few days and commend you for what you have accomplished."

He heard some grumblings echo through the circular chamber. That last line was clearly exaggerated, and they were all aware that he only said it to try to make them feel better. They all knew that they had accomplished nothing and had little to show for it while their constituents continued to starve outside these walls.

"I know that we have not, nor will we ever come to a conclusion on one course of action. But we must move forward with something."

Turning to the governor beside him he said, "Thougus, please review the current front runner options and rank them, somehow. Create a design matrix, vote on popularity, or whatever else you think is best. I trust your judgement. Select the top three and tell me what you need to implement them immediately. We'll try them out, analyze the results, and see if we can turn this situation around."

The dragons all looked from one another, not sure what to do. Odagda looked from dragon to dragon, wondering what they were waiting for. Breaking decorum and entertained by the thought of displaying his implied and well-proven dominance over the others, he gripped the edge of the stone table with his claws, lowered his head, and belched a torrent of flames over the heads of the congregation. A flutter of wings and whipped tails flurried his vision as they darted for the exit to the chamber and disappeared from view.

The dragon grinned a toothy smile, bobbed his head in satisfaction, and turned to go back to his personal chambers to dine with his awaiting wife.

For the next two solar cycles, his inner circle worked tirelessly to finalize their proposals, inventory available resources to determine what was feasible, and brought in key subject matter experts from among the citizenry to give testimony to the plans. Odagda called them back into the chamber and listened to their presentations.

After several long hours of proposals, background investigation reports, and reviewing the plans with their peers, the council elected to move forward with the following three selections.

Plan A involved a combination of parallel path improvement projects to the agricultural sectors. If they could get more crops to grow, then they could supply the dragons with more fruits, vegetables, and grain products to rapidly boost their food supplies. Additionally, the crops would then help to feed livestock which would in turn provide the populace with an influx of meat.

Plan B focused around educating the dragons of their nation on how to better balance their daily meals and move away from a meat centric diet.

If crops could be increased from the activities under Plan A, then hopefully enough citizens would be converted under Plan B to take advantage of those gains. Nobody was entirely confident that this would work given their long and storied history of consuming the flesh of their kills for both pleasure and sustenance, but it was worth a shot.

And lastly, Plan C sought to encourage ambitious citizens to venture out from the populated areas to explore and settle the outlying regions away from the capital.

The thought was that if a significant portion of the dragon population could move into the unknown regions of the planet and live more heavily off of the land itself, then they would reduce the burden on the food supply within the established areas. These dragons would be given a number of perks to entice them to move out and stay out there, hopefully giving the capitol region a long-term gain on their absence.

As the last of the dragons finished their presentations, they quietly took their seats and looked to Odagda for a response. The elder dragon sat motionless for several long minutes before replying. These were ambitious plans with little to no way to guarantee that any of them would work. Each plan required a substantial number of financial resources and time to implement. If a key aspect of any plan failed to produce positive results for the teams, it would be too late to try something else and they'd have little to no remaining resources to try a second attempt.

They needed to do it right, and they needed to do it right now.

Rising from his seat, Odagda slowly looked around the room and made eye contact with each of his fellow dragons, one by one. They had done a good job considering all that was working against them, and he would be remiss to not acknowledge it.

"Thank you, all of you," Odagda began. "I know that this was difficult, and you have had your backs up against the cave for quite some time now. I like your final plans and think that they have a high probability of success. Please work with your team leaders and don't leave any stones unturned as you dive into the scope of the work. Do whatever it takes and don't hesitate to request any funding and materials you may need. Time is our enemy here, and I intend to beat it."

The group stared back at him, exhausted and not sure where to begin. But they would do it or else resign themselves to watch their friends and family starve to death.

With a final nod, Odagda gave them their leave.

"Dismissed."

After the plume of fire and finally died down and he was able to extinguish the flames licking his chamber walls, Odagda circled his scorched dining room table and bent down to look at the smaller dragon hiding beneath.

"Jordana, please come out. I am sorry," the elder implored the younger of the two. "Please, take your seat and tell me again."

The still-shaken quartermaster for the city of Calderopolis nodded in agreement and emerged from her temporary shelter. As the last of her previous sentence had left her teeth, Odagda roared in anger and shot fire in her general direction. He had never been a violent dragon before, but the past six months had changed him considerably.

Taking her seat, she settled in and started again. "Sir, Governor Thougus is dead."

The words hung in the air between the two of them for what felt like eternity. Odagda's lifelong friend and political ally was gone. He had been the last line of defense between him and the frustrated dragons of the region.

"What happened?"

"The governor, Chief Toudall, and I went down to the market this morning to meet with guild leaders," Jordana continued. "It was a routine meeting where we simply discuss that week's inventory levels, the general mood of the populace, price minimums and maximums to enforce on all the vendors, and other typically boring business details. We've done this every week for six months with no prior cause for concern."

"So how was today different?" Odagda asked.

"Typically, when we arrive," she began, "there's nobody there to even care about our presence and we easily make our way to whatever store we're congregating in that day. We choose a different site each time to minimize the burden on any particular store while also giving each vendor an equal chance to cater the meeting and show off their goods.

"This time, however, was different. Upon arrival at the grain warehouse chosen for today's meeting, we were met with a crowd of dragons circling the building. It was clear from the onset that they were on the verge of violence and simply awaiting a catalyst to set them off. They were roaring, um, let's say 'unpleasantries', towards the proprietor, and in turn, us."

"So, what in the name of Morrigan happened then?" Odagda uttered, the tension rising in his voice to an unsettling magnitude. It was rare to hear of a murder in the capital, let alone of a government official. The loss of his friend and colleague had hit close to home.

"As we attempted to make our way through the crowd, several of the protesters began to launch salvos of fire into the air," Jordana resumed. "It was a little unnerving at the time, I'll admit, but in retrospect, it was clear that they were just angry and trying to make their point. I don't think that anyone meant physical harm to any amongst our group beyond a singed ego and dignity. But as we approached the warehouse, a worker opened the main entrance and a gust of air escaped. We couldn't see it at the time, but a witness described a cloud of grain dust flowing outward into the warm morning air. As you probably know, the dust is extremely flammable, and it must have caught a gout of fire from one of the protestors."

Jordana paused to let that sink in. Any dragon with common sense probably knew what happened next, but she needed a moment to calm herself, and judging by the expression on Odagda's face, so did he.

"We never really saw the blast as much as we felt the ground hit us first," she continued. "It happened so fast that we were on the ground before we had any idea of what was going on. The shockwave leveled the thin-walled warehouse and set most of the surrounding buildings on fire within seconds. Most of us were simply thrown to the dirt and suffered minor burns to our scales, but Thougus... Governor Thougus, he was hit with the remains of a structural beam from the warehouse and..." Jordana trailed off, not finishing the thought.

Odagda didn't need her to. The fate of their friend was clear enough. He thanked her for the update, apologized once again for almost setting her on fire for the second time that day, and dismissed her for the day. She was rattled enough already and needed some time to herself. Walking back to his chair, he slumped down into the hard stone seat and stared out the window of his chamber.

Over the next few months, the citizens of Mars carried on as they had for years. They ate, worked, kept the cities and towns operational, and tried to live a relative semblance of normalcy, if you discounted the massive food shortage and declining health of the populace.

Food supplies continued to dwindle for the average citizen, workers from every field across the board became sluggish and less productive, and many dragons began to die from malnourishment and starvation. The more well-to-do dragons of the population fared better thanks to industry connections and more disposable income, but the poor grew poorer and couldn't afford to pay the exorbitant prices of goods on the market thanks to greedy vendors overinflating prices. Fights among hungry dragons grew more frequent and general calls from the masses for help from the government persisted.

Odagda and his task force continued to monitor the daily reports from across the land with grim enthusiasm. The population steadily grew as more dragon families continued to reproduce and add to their numbers. While some dragons were dying at historically normal rates due to old age and a variety of common diseases and injuries, not enough were dying to balance out the increases.

It was this last thought which Odagda found himself contemplating one morning, disgusted with himself. While pragmatically he needed people to die to balance out the continuous births and longer life spans of his citizenry, the numbers just weren't there. The logical half of his brain was able to review the numbers without feeling emotional about the callous goal of watching a larger rate of his fellow dragons die each day, but his more tender, emotional side just couldn't bear it. He needed to save them all. Yet their traditions, improved medical care, and culinary preferences stood in his way.

Reading the daily updates, he skimmed through some of the drier, data-heavy sections to get to what he needed. Scanning his slitted eyes over the executive summary from the city's key dietician, he saw that on average the general populace of dragons continued to reject a more plant-based diet. They were literally and figuratively burning through the remaining herds of livestock. Without stringent intervention on the government's part, the meat-producing industries would dry up completely within a few months as the animals were driven to the brink of extinction.

Over the course of the next year, Odagda tried everything that he and the committee could come up with. They promoted the consumption of even more extreme options to the hungry masses: lab-grown meats, less edible plants, and naturally found fruits & vegetables not typically consumed. They even tried different grain variants not typically harvested due to poor taste or nutritional value, among many others. And still the dragons complained.

Fighting down in the markets grew more frequent with each passing day. News reports came across his desk of dragons stealing from each other and breaking into homes to rob the owners of food. Some desperate souls were even sneaking into the local schools to loot the cafeterias of anything of value before the whelps could eat it.

Odagda had never seen his people drop to such lows and he could hardly believe his eyes and ears. Each story was worse than that before it, more unbelievable and sickening to bear witness to.

His dragons were not barbarians. They were refined, intelligent creatures at the top of the food chain. The leadership, his leadership, should have seen this coming long ago and taken necessary actions earlier on to prevent such a catastrophe. How had he slipped so far from his previous managerial glory to his current position?

He had nobody to blame but himself.

Steepling his clawed hands together below his snout, he allowed himself a moment of respite to lean his muscular jaw downward and closed his eyes. While not very supportive nor relaxing, the tiny instance of quiet solitude gave him the clarity which he needed. If he couldn't sway the masses from bringing about their own demise, perhaps he could help the next generation of dragons avoid their fate.

Lurching up from his stone chair, he ran the length of the chamber and veered towards the launch window at the end. Unfurling his massive wings, he stretched them outward and pumped them once, twice, and a third time as he neared the edge. Running as fast as he could, he dove for the opening and glided out into the cool evening air.

Moving about the dark cavern deep within the hillside, Aenfrey moved from egg to egg as she had thousands of times this day alone. Day after day, week after week, not even the gods knew how many times she had gone through this ritual of hers. It was her duty, and hers alone, to oversee the care and development of all eggs on the planet of Mars.

Carefully inspecting each egg in turn, she gently lifted the precious object from its holder and held it aloft before the sacred Flame of Truth. Placing the egg between the flame and her eyes, she could inspect the tiny whelp frozen in stasis within the protective shell. She looked for signs of improper growth of the tiny being inside, cracks or flaws in the shell itself, and anything else of concern which may arise through the natural process of the dragon heart transforming into the body of the next generation of dragon.

Placing the egg back into the holder, she went to grab the next egg in line when she heard a flurry of footsteps and the soft swishing of a dragon's tail along the smooth stone floor of her chamber.

Listening intently, she was able to pick out the characteristic gait of the approaching dragon. He had visited her many times over the years to inquire as to the health of his dragons, but never in such a hurried manner. Something must be wrong, she thought to herself.

Gently turning from her spot along the rack of eggs, her eyes met his as he rounded the corner in a rush. Leader Odagda.

"Lady Aenfrey," the leader began, the air pumping in and out of his tired lungs as he settled his body from the rapid transit across the city. "My apologies for the late hour and the unceremonious entrance."

"No need for apologies, sir," she replied, truthfully. "You are always welcome here and we know that you have many duties on your docket."

"We?" he queried.

Looking around, she stretched out her arms and wings to take in the long chamber and innumerous halls shooting off into the distance. "The eggs and I."

"Oh, well, yes," he replied, flustered. Whether or not the embryos of the developing whelps counted as living dragons or not was a heated debate that spanned a millennium, but he understood her point and moved onward. "I must speak with you at once. Is now a good time?"

Moving to her dining room, the two dragons sat at her humble stone table and poured the first of many cups of herbal tea. He posited their dilemma and what they had tried over the past year, all of which she was painfully familiar, and what their current options were. She nodded with each one, holding back her opinions until the leader had his say.

Growing up in a highly patriarchal society, she knew that it would not do well to interrupt the dragon while he spoke. But she also knew that once he got his words in and felt heard, that she could weigh in heavily and push him around if needed.

Today was not that kind of day, though. What he said was as dire as he made it sound, and their options were poorly limited. She only saw merit in one plan, and she could tell that it was solely the one for which he had traveled here tonight. They both clearly despised the plan yet clung to it as their last vestige of salvation. The dragons of Mars could not be saved. It was time for the next clutch of eggs to take their rightful place in their species' history.

After another pot of tea, the leader rose from the table and thanked Aenfrey for her wisdom and precious time. Grimly nodding as he turned to take his leave, he bolted down the hallway as the sounds of his footsteps followed and disappeared after him. No sound came from his tail as he was running too quickly for the appendage to even touch the floor in the wake of his flight.

Letting out a heavy sigh which she had been holding in for the better part of an hour, Aenfrey dropped heavily onto the bench beside her. Leaning her head back into the wall, she gazed lazily down the hallway to where her slumbering dragons awaited her care and attention. Little did they know that she was about to toss their lives to the wind, sailing into the void on hopes and dreams alone.

Several weeks later, on a cool morning, Odagda approached the lectern and faced his constituents. That is, the small number who had even bothered to show up. As the food shortage issues exploded and news of turmoil rippled across the lands, the average dragon's opinion of him and their government had rapidly dwindled as of late. On a good day, he was met with little more than casual indifference from his people. On a bad day, well, there had been some bad days.

Many dragons had abandoned their homes and jobs within the city proper to head out into the unsettled lands in search of naturally found food and a simpler way of life. On several occasions, some groups of disenfranchised citizens had tried to overthrow the government and seat their own leadership. Thankfully, each plot had been foiled by his guards or his fellow dragons stopping their brethren before it was too late.

He still had faithful beings within the populace, and many gave him the benefit of the doubt. He had gotten them this far, after all, and he deserved their respect.

Which is what made today's announcement so hard.

He updated the small crowd on that day's death toll and the status of incoming food supplies from nearby farms. There had even been reports coming in about instances of cannibalism amongst his people. Dragons turning on dragons, eating their own kind... it completely disgusted him. Survival was one thing, but this was madness.

Again, he pleaded with them to ration their foodstuffs, decrease meat consumption, and to try new and unusual foods. Once again, his words fell on deaf ears. Even as he continued to speak, he heard multiple voices in the crowd interrupt and shout out to be heard.

"Where's our meat?!"

"I'm not eating plants! That's the food that my food eats!"

"I'm sick of grains! Give us beef! Where's the beef?!"

Placing his claws upon his face, he pressed his palms against his eyes and rubbed them across his weary scales to the temples of his skull. Trying to will the pressure away which had been building within his brain for the past year, he knew that the move would make him appear weak in the eyes of his opponents. He didn't care anymore. His leadership, re-election, his legacy... none of it mattered if he couldn't safeguard his species.

Clearing his throat, he began, "I have but one remaining option, then. Working with the hatchery will provide a means of escape for our next generation. It is clear that the dragons of Mars no longer care about their own survival, or else we would have made drastic planet-wide changes years ago. We have doomed ourselves, and soon shall pay the price for our arrogance and ambivalence."

The crowd, stunned by his words, remained uncharacteristically silent. It wasn't until he quickly turned from his spot on the stage and exited through a nearby portal in the stone wall that the dragons roared in confusion and contempt.

Racing from the sounds of outrage and bellowing flames, he made his way to the hatchery to oversee the next steps. He had failed his people, but there may still be time to redeem the next generation.

Blasting out of the doorway exiting the building, he stretched his wings and flew straight to Aenfrey. If he was lucky, she would soon be finished with her part of the plan, and they could hopefully execute the scheme prior to any dragons coming to stop them.

He wasn't sure if anyone really cared what they did with the eggs, but he wasn't going to leave anything to chance. Pumping his wings faster, he rose in altitude until he found himself within a strong gust of wind heading in the general direction of his destination. Riding the wind, he soared to the hatchery and mentally prepared himself for what would come next.

Standing outside of the massive iron door, Odagda knocked again on the hard surface. Feeling drops of cool water on the scales of his head, he looked up to see a light sprinkle started. As if he had needed another reminder of his dismal mood. Not hearing anything from the other side of the portal, he was about to rap his muscled claws against the door when he finally heard the screech of iron-on-iron as the locking bolt was slid sideways. Part of him wanted to go find some oil and lubricate the metal for her, but there were bigger problems to address first. Old habits die hard, they say.

Stepping back as the door opened, he smiled as he saw the face of his old friend emerge from the darkness.

"How may I help you, sir?" Aenfrey answered upon seeing him.

"Good evening, friend," Odagda stated solemnly. "It is time."

Without another word, the two shuffled into the entrance and locked the door behind them. The time for public discourse, voting, and governmental transparency was over. He had tried to help the dragon race save itself, but they were cemented to their traditions and would clearly never change. Some bent and did their best to adapt to the new normal of the times, but they were not plentiful enough to make any real change in the whole of their society. The Sun was setting on the time of the Dragons of Mars, and it was up to him to ensure their society's continuation.

Marching through the end of the tunnel from the main portal, the two dragons emerged into the large work chamber within the mountain. Allowing his limbs and wings to fully stretch upon entering the grand room, he took in the sight before him. A dozen egg servants of Aenfrey's team were arrayed around the perimeter, each standing nearby a pallet of eggs carefully arranged in protective trays and racks.

Pallet loaders were waiting off to the side near the exit to the room, and he could hear the exhaust system already running in the circular opening in the rock above their heads.

Everything was prepared.

Scanning the dragons assembled before him, he allowed himself the slightest of smiles. Not a smile derived from happiness, but one from acceptance of the situation before him and a feeling of hard-earned contentment based on the least vile of available options.

"Thank you, all of you," he addressed the collective. "I know that many of our fellow dragons disagree with me on this course of action, and I may very well be dooming our race on this planet. Those of you who agree with me, including yourselves, may very well be a simple echo chamber which I'm operating within and make me feel that I'm doing the right thing. I will be the first to admit that I do not know the right thing to do at this moment, but I feel that action is better than inaction. History will judge me accordingly, and I am prepared for whatever sentence awaits me."

The silence in the room slammed into him harder than the expected roars of dissent that he was used to as of late. He didn't know if they were silent because they agreed, or disagreed, with him and were afraid to speak up in public, albeit a small gathering, or if they were still processing the ramifications of what he had just said. He may never find out the truth of the matter. Nonetheless, it was time to work.

"You have all been briefed on the plan by Madam Aenfrey and know what you must do," he continued. "Finish your preparations and we will begin as soon as possible."

With that, he gently bowed, thanked them for their time and took his leave from the mountain.

Flying as fast as his wings would take him, he travelled directly to the home of his lead geology scientist. It wouldn't bother to meet at this lab or test facilities. He only needed confirmation of data, not a demonstration or experiment. Coming in hot, he billowed out his wings and shot his feet forward to alight on the edge of the scientist's balcony. Gently hopping down to the stone pavers, he let out a friendly roar of greeting and rapped his claws against the stone entryway.

Hearing the sounds, the owner of the home quickly made his way out to the visitor. "My lord, it is good to see you," Morrifrey greeted Odagda.

"You, as well, my friend," Odagda uttered in between breaths. "May I have your attention for a moment?"

"Of course, of course. Come in."

The two dragons entered the male's humble living quarters. A longtime member of the scientific community, Morrifrey had devoted his life to studying Mars, the dragons and their effect on the planet, and their place within the stars. Morrifrey was a font of knowledge tail lengths beyond Odagda's understanding, and the leader had come to rely upon his old friend many times throughout his time in government.

"Did you get my last letter?" Odagda asked when they were safely inside and away from any prying eyes or attentive ears.

"Yes. About that..." Morrifrey replied, the tension in his voice hiding little. "I am not quite sure what to make of it. What are you trying to do, exactly?"

"Why are you confused, my friend?" Odagda asked, a smirk creeping across his face. It was hard to see, but a small twinkle in his eye shone through the exhaustion and stress pouring from his gaze. "I thought that my queries were quite straightforward."

"So, you really want to..."

"Yes."

"In a volcano?"

"Well, at least eight, but yes," Odagda replied.

"To transport..." Morrifrey couldn't bear to finish the thought, the mere mention of it made him sick to his stomach.

"Yes," Odagda replied after a moment. "It's the only way. I've exhausted all other rational options. The dragons won't change their ways; we keep reproducing at steady rates; and the planet will no longer be able to sustain our numbers. Hell, it can't sustain us all now. We must do something before the populace begins to devour itself in a final act of brutal survivalism."

"Then, yes," Morrifrey conceded, a heavy sigh filling the air between them. "Yes, it should work. But you must match the diameters properly with a considerable amount of press fit. You must build a proper magnitude of back pressure in order to achieve escape velocity, or the entire cluster will fall back to the surface and destroy the entire lot."

Turning to his desk, he shuffled through a stack of parchment as he searched for his calculations. Thrusting the sought-after collection of papers towards his leader, he proffered his solution to the elder dragon.

It was an unthinkable action, only seeming rational in his brain if carried out with utmost care, testing, and engineered optimal efficiency to ensure that every life was given the chance to succeed.

Odagda graciously accepted the bundle and began skimming through the seemingly endless supply of data and simulated scenarios. Morrifrey had been busy.

"Thank you, Morrifrey," Odagda said, bowing. "You have been my most loyal servant throughout the years, and you may have just single-clawedly saved our species."

Without another word, Odagda walked through the doorway to the edge of the balcony, pushed off with his legs, and soared through the air.

Watching him take to the wind and quickly disappear into the blinding light of the setting Sun, Morrifrey looked in upon himself and questioned his contribution to this madness.

"...or doomed it."

Pouring fire through his aching mouth, Odagda watched in exhausted satisfaction as the crystalline bar of quartz began to soften within the crucible. Pulling hot ambient air in through his nostrils, he pushed onward and drove wave after wave of flaming power into the ceramic-reinforced vessel held by his assistant. Letting off for a second to catch his breath, he was elated to see that the softening bar had just begun to liquify beneath his continued onslaught.

"Quickly! Give me the—" he barked at the dragon next to him at their station. He couldn't think of the right word and simply snapped his fingers in the direction of the tool. He hadn't meant to sound so forceful, but they had been at this all day, and he was losing the fervent enthusiasm which had driven him through most of the agony of today's efforts. His brain was muddled, oxygen deprived, and simply exhausted.

"Sir!" the assistant replied, quickly handing the long-handled crucible to his leader, knowing what the elder dragon wanted.

"Thank you," he said, making an effort to soften his tone. "Now, gently tighten the clamps as I begin to pour. We don't want to mess this up like last time."

The assistant drooped his head, clearly still contemplating his previous errors and carrying the shame with him throughout the day.

Sighing, Odagda shook his head and continued. He would need to buy this one a drink after and formally apologize. He wasn't being a good leader, let alone a good friend. He had very few dragons on his side at this point and couldn't afford to alienate any more than he already had.

"I am sorry, young one," he said to the assistant, who quietly listened without saying a word. He couldn't tell if the dragon was afraid of him and his position, angered by the outlash, or just equally half-asleep and doing his best to remain on his own two feet. "Let's finish this pod and call it a day."

With a nod from the younger male, Odagda belched out another sustained salvo of fire into the cooling mass within the crucible, waited for it to slowly change color and consistency. Eyeing the material, he knew by now how to look for just the right signs of readiness and began to pour. The two dragons worked together to fill the gaps between each ovoid with the liquified quartz. The rapidly thickening material slowed as it travelled through the amalgamation, finding home deep within the ball and coming to a stop. Letting the final drop of mineral fall from the crucible, Odagda returned the tool to the rack to cool off and stepped back to inspect their work. Pacing around the perimeter of their creation, he nodded in satisfaction. Rounding the mass, stopping several times to crouch and carefully examine a detail here and there, the clearly proud dragon slapped the assistant on the back of the wings and nodded.

"Nice job. Drinks are on me."

Struggling to lift their feet, the two shuffled their way out of their designated workshop and made their way to the mess hall. Refueling their parched throats with the promised liquids, Odagda bid the other dragon a good day and dismissed him from the day's service. Walking the main thoroughfare around the large chamber, he poked his head into several other alcoves to see how they were doing. Noticing a blur of motion at the other end of the room, he recognized the blur's owner and made his way down the length of the hall.

"Aenfrey," the elder dragon called out, calmly. "How fares thee?"

She shushed him and held up a single claw. Few dragons could get away with this level of indifference toward their leader, and Aenfrey was one of them. Knowing what she was going through, Odagda patiently waited until she was done. It was his fault, after all, that she was going nuts right now.

Looking up from her slate a few moments later, the dragon let out a long breath which she had forgotten she had been holding.

"My lord, my apologies," Aenfrey began. "It's just been a long day. We have six pods at or near completion, thankfully. One was damaged during the melting process and needs to be reworked.

Hopefully the wee beings inside the eggs were not damaged, but we won't know until we inspect them. We may never know until it's too late. I have half the reporters in Calderopolis milling about outside wondering why there's smoke billowing from our chimneys for the first time in eons. We should really put some kind of buffer on top of those, you know," she said, scribbling a note down on her slate. "Jordana's riding my wings questioning why I'm stripping the city's supplies of quartz crystals for our little project, claiming that she should be the one to make the call as to where and how they're used and not some pompous bureaucrat."

She looked up as she finished the quote from Jordana. "Sorry, nothing personal; she's just fired up, you know? And I have a bevy of assistants who have never done this work before and are overworked and stressed out and need a break and can't figure out why the work isn't going as planned and keep coming to me for help and I don't know what to do for them. I mean, I'm an egg caretaker. I've never done this before!"

Reaching out with his claws, he gently gripped Aenfrey by the shoulders. "Aenfrey, I am sorry to see you so anxious. You're doing an amazing job." He nodded his head in agreement with his words, hoping to convince her of their veracity. "I mean it," he said, waving a claw around the room. "All of this— look at it— is all because of you and your skills. Whatever gets done will be great. I promise you."

Gripping her slate with his hand, he delicately removed it from her tightly held grasp and gave it a quick scan. "We seem to be right on track and will be done soon. We just wrapped up another pod in my work cell and the others are close behind."

Her shoulders slumped as if a heavy burden had just been lifted from them. She had been running solely on adrenaline and tea for so long that he could physically see the stress, albeit only a little, drain from her body at his words.

"Thank you, my lord."

"Why don't you go rest, and I'll send for you when needed," he said. "We have this under control."

She hesitated for a moment, but after he continued to stare down the length of his snout, she ultimately relented and left the building for the first time in days.

Watching her shuffle away in resigned acceptance, he waited until she was out of sight to lean back against the wall. Letting his head hit the smooth stone, he slumped to the floor and wrapped his wings around his body. It wouldn't do to let his subjects see him so weak, but he was spent. He couldn't recall when he had last eaten, and it had been at least a day and a half since he had last slept. He was running on fumes and needed to rest.

Coaxing life from his aching leg muscles, he forced himself to his feet and walked towards the nearest work cell. Talking with each team of artisans, he dismissed them for the night and ordered them all to go home and rest for two days. If they kept running as they were, mistakes were bound to happen, or someone would get hurt. Following the last dragon to leave, he closed the temple door behind him and flew off into the distance to see his queen.

One week later, the team of dragons stood in the main chamber of the temple, cheerfully taking in the majestic sight of their efforts. Eight pods were collected and placed on careful display, one for each of the major planetoids in their surrounding sector of space. It was sad to see the precious entities being used as such, but this was possibly their only path for survival.

Leaving the side of Aenfrey, Odagda walked the length of the hall until he found Morrifrey busy at work. He had spent the morning inspecting each pod and verifying that they were ready for the next phase of the plan.

"So, how do they look?" Odagda inquired of his friend.

Picking himself up off the floor where he had been laying on his back to inspect the underside of the adjacent pod, the dragon seer dusted himself off.

"Well, my lord," he began, "aside from being the most absolutely insane idea that any dragon has ever had in the history of dragons—at least the dragons here on Mars—they look good enough."

"Good enough?" Odagda asked with a slight tilt of his head to get a better look at the dragon before him.

"May I speak openly, sir?"

"I would expect nothing less."

"Sir," Morrifrey began, "I'm just not sure about any of the math behind this plan of yours. We haven't verified that sufficient pressure can be built up within each volcano; how well the pods will seal the opening; what level of thrust is achievable; or if the pods themselves will be destroyed in the process. We don't know if one pod firing before the others will drain the system pressure within the planet enough to cause a drop in pressure for the other pods. The magma system's hydraulic properties have not been sufficiently tested to determine max and min pressure and volumetric characteristics to decide whether or not each volcano is ready, and safe, to launch. We don't know if the explosions will have any adverse effects on us here on the surface nor the environment itself."

"Is that all?"

The seer stared at his leader in disbelief. "Maybe? I don't know. I'm getting frazzled just trying to process all of these variables. This has never been done before in our known history. An undertaking of this magnitude has never even been dreamt of. If you actually pull this off, you'll either go down in history as a genius or a crackpot."

Odagda stared back at the seer and slowly blinked once.

"No offense," Morrifrey quickly offered once he saw the elder dragon's expression. "Sir."

"None taken, obviously," Odagda replied, smirking. "What do you need from me in order to get a warm and fuzzy feeling about all of this?"

The seer stared back at him, an unreadable expression on his face. "Well, we should lay out what can be tested and what can't. Then try our damnedest to ignore the latter and do what we can for the former."

"Anything you need, just name it," Odagda stated, trying to

reassure his friend. "This is the most important thing that our species may ever attempt. We need to do it correctly; we'll only get one shot at this."

And so, the two dragons drafted a plan on their slates and formulated some test protocols. They couldn't properly test the internal pressure of the magma system within the planet, so that was immediately taken off the list. It would also be nearly almost impossible to determine if any negative effects would be wrought upon the environment as the massive scale of the undertaking was unprecedented. Their mathematical models simply didn't have the necessary historical evidence to sufficiently account for all outcomes. What they could do, however, was to construct a test pod of similar size, composition, and density to a real pod and test fire it from a volcano. Working with their team, they gathered minerals from the mountain of similar volume and density and carefully constructed a prototype.

Two days later, the team stepped back and inspected their work. In the middle of the chamber sat the mockup which would be their test pod. Extra care had been taken to ensure that the melted welds in between each egg had bonded properly and that the cluster was solid. Additionally, more quartz crystals than needed for the welds had been warmed and the resultant lava-esque goo was slathered around the entire surface of the pod. Upon cooling, the extra quartz had created a thick and exceptionally durable claw-length coating enveloping the conglomeration in a natural suit of armor. It was the hope of the team that this would help the pod survive the insertion into the volcano and the subsequent violent forces and stresses experienced by the object in the next phase of their plan.

Measuring the final diameter of the object, Odagda had sent craftsdragons off ahead of the team with their as-built data in tow to begin honing the inner diameter of their target location for the initial test. If this were going to work, they'd need to minimize their tolerances on all aspects of the pod and volcano's opening to maximize the resultant thrust.

Nothing like this had ever been tried before, and even Odagda was beginning to have his doubts.

With the advance team off and running, the remaining crew carefully loaded the pod onto a massive carrier sled and secured it in place for the journey ahead. Tapping several of the strongest dragons from the amongst the personnel, Odagda ordered them to head out at once and drag the test pod out to the test volcano. The few who were now behind ran through seismic charts, recent tectonic activity on their continent, and double checked their math. Then checked it again.

After running the numbers once more, the ever-fastidious Odagda gathered his research materials and flew out to a mountain adjacent to the target volcano. Accompanying him were Morrifrey, Aenfrey, and a select group of trusted assistants to help him monitor the event and document the results. By the time that they had arrived, everything had been prepared at the target site and the other dragons were in position, awaiting his command.

With a mighty roar, he signaled the craftsdragons to lower the pod into place within the opening of the volcano.

All dragons retreated to the nearby cliff faces and mountainsides to watch the next few minutes unfold. Given the active nature of this volcano, they didn't need to wait very long.

Watching the top of the volcano begin to rumble, several of the dragons shielded their faces with their wings. Not Odagda. The dragon watched as the experiment began and was not phased in the slightest as the explosion rocked the valleys below. He braced himself against the shockwave, turning his head skyward as the pod rocketed forth from the belly of the mountain. He stared skyward for a long time, watching and waiting for signs of their imminent failure but it never came.

A toothy grin spread across his face as he looked to the dragons surrounding him, anxiously waiting for him to speak.

"That'll do," he said before leaping from the mountainside and soaring back to the egg chambers to continue their work.

One week later, Odagda stood on the stage of the largest open-air amphitheater within Calderopolis. He was originally going to give this address inside one of the meeting halls within the governmental buildings at the center of the capital, but he wanted to give every dragon an equal opportunity to hear what he needed to say.

Looking up at the seats surrounding him, he was awestruck by the turnout. Every seat in the arena had been packed wing to wing by his constituents, with many hovering above in an attempt to see and hear their leader. Times had been rough, and they were only going to get worse. The dragons needed to hear something optimistic.

Which is why he had decided to change his speech at the last moment. He had planned to deliver a fire and brimstone laden diatribe of near-insults and reprimands, lecturing his fellow dragons on their selfishness and lack of will to ensure the survival of the greater good. They had been given clear directions from the scientific community as to how to prevent the ruin of their very planet, their only home in the solar system. And yet, they had thrown away any chance of success by carelessly barreling down the wrong path, leading their civilization into further turmoil with only themselves to blame.

But he couldn't deliver that speech. Not now, and possibly not ever. For a rant was not what they needed, nor what he had the heart to deliver at this point. Too much had transpired and many of their troubles had far surpassed the point of no return.

Or perhaps, it was his heart that led him to this morning's proclamation. He would lie to them. He would tell them only good news and leave out the bad. Those who understood the implications of his delivery had most likely already figured out the truth of the matter and it wouldn't change a thing. Those who couldn't comprehend, or refused to believe the message which he was about to put forth, would hear the positivity within the message and do what they wished with the narrative. Either way, the future of the dragons of Mars was out of his hands. The future of dragonkind, however, would fall to the leadership of the next generation.

"My fellow dragons!" he bellowed at the top of his lungs. "I called you here today to witness the next phase in dragon civilization. Long have we called Mars our home while ignoring our planetary neighbors in the cold void of space."

He paused to give the dragons a chance to listen and comprehend his words. He wanted them to picture space exploration and conquering new lands to spread their species amongst the stars. He wanted them to grasp on to that sense of wonder and excitement before contemplating the dark side to the plan.

"Our team has put together a series of exploration vessels capable of delivering the next generation of our kind to lands of wonder beyond our planetary confinement. The other planets surrounding our star shall no longer remain barren to dragonkind and shall harbor the continued growth and flourishment of our species.

"I give you our dragonauts!"

Turning to his assistant, he motioned for the dragon to signal the others. The younger dragon turned his head skyward and belched a long, thin plume of fire toward the azure sky. Watching with satisfaction as the assistants placed every mile or so from the stage continued the fire plume procession, one after another branched out in eight different directions towards the volcanos awaiting in the distance. As the teams at each site saw the message being relayed to their respective positions, they released the clamp mechanisms holding the egg pods above the openings of their crater cone. As one, the pods dropped into position and lodged themselves into the finely honed openings, sealing off the blistering magma and super-heated gases below.

Odagda motioned for the onlookers to join him in turning towards their nearest volcano, prepared to personally witness the salvation of their kind. Retrieving a magnified sight tube from the lectern before him, he extended the device and peered through the small opening. Fixing his gaze upon the group assembled at the top of the crater, he watched as they dove from the hot air surrounding them and raced away from the building pressure bomb which they had just created.

He was concerned about using any of his dragons to carry out this task, but it was ultimately decided to be the only way to guarantee success. Even their best remote trigger mechanisms were unpredictable in high temperature environments and the team couldn't risk a failed launch on any of the pods. The assistants triggering the individual pod drops were selected from a pool of dedicated volunteers who knew the ins and outs of the project, as well as the inherent risks involved. While none of their team would want to see something bad occur during this momentous occasion, they all knew the possible outcomes should they fail in their mission.

As if the very planet itself were listening to Odagda's innermost thoughts and fears, the now-plugged volcanos began to unleash their bottled-up potential energy. Several of the peaks that had been actively spewing torrents of lava through their main vents triggered almost immediately, taking the attendant crews by surprise. One of the volcanos, in fact, launched salvos of orange rock-melting destruction over the wingtips of one of the teams not moving quickly enough. The dragons bellowed as the heat singed their scales and taught them to move with more haste. Many pushed past each other, desperately clamoring for any path to escape the inferno.

One by one, the volcanoes unleashed the pressurized lava from their vents before violently hurling the blockages skyward with mind-numbing magnitudes of force.

Working the room and playing the hand which he had been dealt, Odagda roared in celebration as the eight red hot spheres rocketed from the surface of Mars and ascended through the atmosphere. The crowd in general couldn't possibly understand what they had been watching this whole time, but the sight of it all was impressive, nonetheless.

Fiery trails of lava followed in the wake of each pod, shooting an octuplet of ochre-tinged fingers high into the air above. Listening to the reaction of the gathered assembly, Odagda decided to continue onward. He had to tell his fellow dragonfolk what was happening.

"My fellow dragons," he began, "what you have just witnessed is the first step in our exploration of the galaxy beyond our small, planetary home. Long have we looked to the heavens to track the movements of stars and planets, yearning to learn all that we could. We strive to better understand our place in the galaxy and to one day step foot on the surface of another heavenly body.

"As you have just seen, eight pods have left the confines of our planet and were jettisoned into the great beyond. While we do not yet have the technology to afford us the ability to send our own dragonkind into space, we can offer our next generation the ability to grow up on a new world.

"Each one of these pods has been launched on an intercept course with the largest of our solar neighbors. When they land, they will hatch on alien soil and propagate our species into uncharted territory!"

Odagda paused as the crowd, for the most part, began to cheer and roar in triumph. Finding himself short of breath, he inhaled deeply to make up for the oxygen spent during his past few sentences. The action felt labored, though. Pushing the thought aside, he scanned the faces of the dragons closest to him to read their reactions. While a large majority seemed excited by his words and had joined in with the raucous crowd, he could tell that some were not buying it. In an instant, he could see the confusion and concern growing within their minds. The leader could see that he had not fully convinced his dragons and that his next few words would make or break the mood of the city.

He never had the chance. Before he could tell them of the plan to send the soulless eggs into the black of space in hopes of landing on one of their planetary neighbors, Mars rewarded the dragons for their meddling. Even if his scientists could aim or control the thrust from the volcanoes, or remotely guarantee that the eggs would hatch upon impact or let alone survive the journey through the cold vacuum beyond their atmosphere, Odagda and his dragons were doomed. They had stripped and robbed the planet of her resources for too long and it was time to pay their dues.

If any dragon had been paying attention to the individual launches and held themselves back from the excitement and celebratory antics which played out from the planets' first explorative launch, one might have noticed that not everything was going to plan. If there really was one. While eight pods were launched, only seven had actually left the Martian surface. And of those seven, only six left its launch-volcano intact.

Between the concussive sounds blasting the dragons' ears and the spray of lava following in the pods' wakes, most of the dragons were not paying any mind to the launch sites. Only one dragon really cared enough to look to each of the eight.

Odagda, standing in the center of it all while currently being ignored as the onlookers stared to the heavens, quickly scanned each site. The first six looked good and he nodded to himself with each positive viewing. The seventh, however, was gut-wrenching to see. When the blast occurred, the pent-up pressure within the cone, while successfully launching its egg pod spaceward, had ruptured the stress band placed around the circumference of the outer rim of the opening. From what he could see, lava had shot out of several locations around the perimeter and flooded the face of the volcano with burning death. Plants, animal life, the rocks themselves, and everything else in the way had been scorched and liquified as the flowing lava traced its way to the base of the mountain. Looking around, he couldn't locate a single crew member left alive.

Swinging his head around, he looked to the eighth and final cone, hoping to Tiamat that this one had been successful. Pulling his scope from the confines of his satchel, he quickly scanned the face of the volcano for signs of lava and found none. Following the path back up to the edge of the cone's opening, he was able to see the pod still firmly wedged within the stress band. Looking from side to side, he readily located one pod held firmly in its respective cone. Scanning the swirl of wings and tails running amok around the site, he spotted his two friends, Morrifrey and Aenfrey. The latter was kneeling upon the ground, feeling each and every egg with her sensitive claws, examining the pod's occupants for any signs of trouble. The former was running from dragon to dragon, shooing them away from the pod. Zooming in further, Odagda could see the male's face and winced. He had never seen his friend in such emotional distress over one of his projects.

Stowing the scope, Odagda did the only thing that he knew how: help where needed. Taking a running start, he vaulted over the gathered crowd and launched himself into the air. Heading straight for the eighth volcano site, he poured every joule of energy left within his body to his wing muscles, pushing himself faster through the oddly scented air. He felt himself beginning to droop down to the ground and had to consciously put on more speed to stay in the unfamiliar air.

Closing on his friends, he watched in horror as a crack split open before them, the rocky surface of the volcano drifting in opposite directions. White-hot magma shone below the surface, rushing upwards to spit out fiery lava to any dragon nearby. Adjusting his trajectory, Odagda twisted his body and swooped in line with both Morrifrey and Aenfrey. Tensing his arms, he reached, grabbing each one in turn around their waist. Bracing his body to support the extra weight, he pushed off and slowly took to the air just as the rock beneath their feet sank down, disappearing into the molten doom below.

Looking up at her friend in surprise, Aenfrey finally smiled as she realized they were safe. "Thank you, sir! That was a close one. We almost di—"

Quicker than any of them could have seen, the rock surrounding the perimeter of the egg pod cracked and broke away on one side. The pod leaned against the weakened area, drooped, and broke outwards away from the cone. The pressurized magma built up behind the pod burst forth, launching the pod skyward at a low angle, followed by a torrential flood of burning lava. The pod soared through the hot air and over the heads of the onlookers. The crowd screamed in horror as the pod rocketed straight into the heart of the city, colliding with the main administration building.

The lava continued to burst forward, spilling across the face of the volcano and taking everything in its path. Odagda struggled to keep himself and his wounded friends aloft, but his brain was foggy, and his muscles felt so, so tired. Losing altitude with each subsequent flap of his scaley wings, the three dragons drifted back down to the river of lava below and disappeared.

In the moments following the explosion atop the eighth volcano, thousands of dragons were killed. Those who were in the path of the errant pod died on impact as the hulking mass of eggs and quartz slammed into ancient buildings, leveling the edifices instantly and reducing them to rubble. Fires raged across the districts as lava from the eighth volcano, and then the other seven shortly after, made its way down the slopes and into the low-lying habitable planes surrounding the cityscape.

Unbeknownst to any of the dragons present, even those well versed from the scientific community, a variety of gases erupted from the volcanoes along with the lava and ash spewing skyward throughout the rest of the night. While most of the gaseous mixture was perfectly safe water vapor which innocently collected with the ash to create clouds, two of the gases rushing forth would ultimately spell doom for the dragonfolk across the planet. Hydrogen sulfide mingled in the air, rushing forth from the mouths of the launch sites and began to sink to the ground below. Over time, it collected in the cool, low-lying lands surrounding the volcanoes and sat harmlessly awaiting any of the oxygen-dependent species to breathe it in deeply as they slumbered through the night.

Most of the world's dragons never woke, dying quietly in their sleep as the oxygen was pushed upward by the higher-density gas settling in along the habituated areas. A few may have stirred as their lungs fought within their bodies, struggling to breathe in something usable. Many sat quietly, passing calmly as they dreamed of full plates of dinner and warm bellies.

Meanwhile, millions of tons of sulfur dioxide raced to the upper reaches of the atmosphere, mingling in with the normal collection of nitrogen, oxygen, and other gases naturally found at those altitudes. Collecting amongst the normally-present molecules, the new ingredient allowed chlorine to settle, slowly stripping away the protective ozone layer shielding the planet from cosmic rays while controlling the proper level of sunlight to make it to the surface. Over time, the entirety of the ozone layer disappeared and was stripped away from the planet, allowing the surface of Mars to be pummeled with all matter of life-killing rays and particles. Slowly but surely, the plants and animals died, withered, and were blanched from the historical records and the once life-supporting atmosphere disappeared into the aether, never to be seen again.

EIGHT MONTHS LATER OFF THE COAST OF PRESENT-DAY MEXICO...

Lifting their heads from the deep, blue waters of their herd's lake, a pair of apatosaurs lazily rose to their full height. Their jaws working the lush greenery back and forth across the massive molars inside their mouths while streams of cool, crisp water flowed down their bodies. The two dinosaurs ground the vegetation to a moist pulp before swallowing the bits down the long length of their necks. They lazily chewed upon more of the plant matter, taking their fill from the vibrant ecosystem surrounding them.

Turning toward a bright light in the sky, the two looked to each other in confusion. Normally, they would see the sun during the day and the moon, stars, and the occasional planetary reflections at nighttime. This light, though, was unlike anything that they had ever seen before. As the tiny dot brightened and grew in size, they realized that something must be wrong. Climbing from the shoulder deep water, the pair lumbered their way up the shore to where the rest of the herd was grazing on grasses. Bellowing out to their kin, they roused the group and motioned for the sky. Looking up as one, the herd froze, then bolted.

Screams from the creatures rang out along the great valley that they had called home for generations as far back as any of them could remember. They ran and ran, running away from the fireball in the sky. Looking up as their long, heavy legs carried their bulk as fast as it could go, they watched in horror as the fireball flew over their heads and crashed into the ocean before them.

They looked up as a tidal wave of water rose from the once placid body of water, rising higher into the air as it approached. A plume of water, rock, fire, and dirt shot straight into the air as the ground beneath them rocked and bucked this way and that.

And then the world went black.